There's Something about Zante

By

Elise Williams

Following the herd
Down to Greece
On holiday
Love in the '90s
Is paranoid
On sunny beaches
Take your chances

Copyright © 2022 Elise Williams

Elise Williams has asserted her right to be identified as the author of this Work in accordance with the Copyright Designs and Patents Act of 1988.
This e-book novel is a work of fiction. Names and characters are the product of the author's imagination and any resemblance to actual person, living or dead is entirely coincidental.
All rights reserved. No part of this publication may be reproduced, stored in a retrieval system, or transmitted in any form or by any means, electronic, mechanical, photocopying or otherwise, without the prior permission of the copyright owner.

Contents

Prologue

1   Airport hitch

2   Loving it in Laganas

3   Making waves in Kalamaki

4   Island adventures

The back story 1969-1971

5   Present day – Chase to the Venetian Wells

6   All Change and sweet farewells

Note from the author

Who's who

Social media

Novels to date

Prologue

August 1990
Ruby Royle and Adeline Walters
Manchester

Adeline Walters

'Hey Ruby, why the long face?' I ask my cousin, as the elderly waitress scuttles across the parquet flooring of the Victorian tea rooms with our afternoon treats. It's not the trendiest café in Deansgate, by any means, but it's comfortable, cheap and tucked away. The relentless drizzle forms tributaries on the arched window as Ruby finally turns her attention to me. But she looks straight through me as if I don't exist anymore. I wave a coffee-stained menu at her.

'Hey. Earth calling Ruby!' I wave my hand at her and notice her broken and slightly grubby fingernails as she sets her cup down into its saucer.

'Oh, Adeline, sorry about that. I'm miles away.'

'And just where exactly were you, dear cousin?' I question, feeling slightly vexed that I'm not receiving her full attention. It's been a whole year. She's just returned from backpacking in Australia, and I was hoping for a little more enthusiasm on her part.

Besides, she always has an interesting story to tell — usually.

'Come on Ruby. What on earth has gotten into you? Speak to me!' I plead as I pick up my fork and reach over to the centre of the table and retrieve my ample slice of carrot cake.

'Oh, you know what I'm like. I feed off the sun. And since I returned last week, it's done nothing but piss down!' she says with a face as miserable as the weather outside.

'Well, we do live in Manchester — the rain shadow of the Pennines. But yes, I know what you mean to be honest. After all, it is August,' I reply as a soft thud on the window startles me. It's a bedraggled young man, probably homeless, using his hand over his eyes to peer into the café. A few minutes of silence ensues as he shuffles on and I resume eating my cake, feeling slightly guilty, while my cousin continues to push hers around the plate with the dainty fork. And then suddenly, it's as if a fire has been reignited in her cheeks and her vivid blue eyes look my way.

'Let's go away Addie. Just the two of us. Somewhere hot but not too far away. Oh, and somewhere cheapish as I'm strapped for cash and there's little chance, I'll receive any benefits soon!' I find it hard not to lunge across the flimsy table and embrace her. 'Oh, and there's another thing I should tell you,' she adds, bowing her head slightly to one side.
'Go on cousin. What did you really get up to Down Under that you didn't mention in your postcards?'
'I fell in love!' she whispers.

Ruby Royle

'That travel agent is wrong! He called the island Zante,' I explain as I link arms with my best friend and favourite cousin.
'Oh, how come?' Adeline asks, expertly dodging the puddles on the mirrored pavement, as we exit Wanderlust Travel Agency.

'Zakynthos is its official name. The name Zante comes from the Venetian occupation in the 1400's. Then when the French and English invaded the island around the 1800's and were ousted, the island returned to Greece and was renamed Zacynthos, after the son of the legendary Arcadian chief Dardanos.'

'Oh, right ok. So, do we refer to it as Zante or Zakynthos when we get there? And how do you know all this,' she replies with feigned concern as the spray from car tyres drenches our feet and we curse the inconsiderate city drivers.

'Before I met you today, I was early, so I nipped into St Peter's library and read it in a guidebook of the island. You know me I'm a bit anal about doing my research before I travel anywhere new. Oh, and either name is acceptable nowadays, so I take back what I just said about that young lad,'

I reply as she accepts and nods her head, probably wondering why I'm moaning about something that we have no control over when we're trying in vain to keep from being sodden to the skin with this unrelenting drizzle.

In my head I visualise the sun shining down onto Zakynthos which from the map at the library, takes the shape of a bird on a perch or if you rotate it a fraction, an arrowhead. do believe this island is calling us personally, set like a sapphire gemstone in the Ionian Sea, waiting for us with open arms.
I snap out of my reverie as the number 90 bus pulls up and we make our way to the back seat, careful not to brush past the wet coats of fellow passengers. Now it's my turn for the silent treatment as Adeline takes the window seat, wearing her 'pensive' face.

Adeline

I can't believe that I've just agreed and paid for a holiday to this Greek island, Zante or Zakynthos, whatever it's called, without any accommodation! I honestly thought that the baby faced- travel agent with his blond locks flopping like a poodle's bangs, obscuring his eyes, was having us on when he said there was a lack of hotel vacancies on the Greek Islands, but he could do us a great deal on a return flight from Manchester! After I saw Ruby's eyes light up at the prospect of haggling over prices, I left her to it as I knew she'd bag us a bargain. I continued to look up at the vivid blue holiday destination posters adorning the walls, as my mind went into overdrive, thinking the holiday might be a good ruse to slowly introduce my tomboy cousin to some much- needed female grooming. Starting with the nails, I'll book her in for a basic manicure before we leave, as I very much doubt, she's ever had the luxury or interest in having one before. Then I'll somehow persuade her to have the all-important bikini line wax; after all,

there's no need for any stray spiders' legs –
especially on the beach!

I break my silence as I turn my gaze from the back seat window of the double decker bus.
 'So, if the travel agent said there's a shortage of package holidays and we've only got flights booked, what are we going to do about somewhere to stay?' I ask as nonchalantly as I can. Ruby turns her body side on to me as if she's trying to explain something to a toddler.

 'Our flight arrives at 4am in the morning. What I've done in the past is I go from the Arrivals Hall to the Departure Hall and just sit there until public transport starts up. So, I reckon there will be buses around 7am to take us to one of the main resorts in Zakynthos,' she explains as my attention is diverted to the premature wrinkle on her brow as tight as a knitting needle.

'We'll be fine. It'll be an adventure!' The tight frown softens as she places her hand on my shoulder. There really is no point persuading her to go to another travel agent to find any accommodation, so I leave it all in her capable hands. Anyway, what's more important is the question that's been on my lips since nearly choking on my cake crumbs. She beats me to it.

'To be truthful I'm annoyed at myself for letting it happen. It's just too much of a distraction at this time of my life. I promised myself that I wouldn't get involved this time. It's never the same back home.'
'Ruby, you're talking in riddles. Come on. What's eating you?! Just who or what has stolen your heart? Oh, wait, I bet you're going to say you've fallen for a bronzed, Aussie surfer and after this holiday you're flying back to him. Is that why you can't spit it out Ruby?'
'I wish he was an Aussie. I might have been able to persuade him into marriage and then I could have

stayed in that amazing country of ex-convicts for ever and ever. I would insist you come with me though Addie. There's plenty of eligible single men *down under* – especially the brawny sheep shearers. I'll tell you a story about one when I'm not as tired.'

My cousin knows that I'm not as whimsical as she is and with or without the rain, Manchester is my home. However, I smile with her all the same and allow her to continue.

'He's English,' she adds as I cock my head to the side and raise my eyebrows in a gesture that may be perceived as taking the piss. 'And to add insult to injury, he's from Warrington! twenty miles away! There's no comparison is there Addy? I'd rather be able to say I've met someone from Sydney, Brisbane or Perth, don't you think Addie?' The rhetorical questions cease as she allows me to answer.

'Well, they have an IKEA in Warrington. That's a bonus and it would come in handy for when you're looking for furniture for when you get a house together,' I add, knowing full well I've gone too far. Ruby's bus stop is two before mine as she stands up, pulls her thin cagoule around her and widens her eyes before discreetly sliding two fingers up the side of her face. It's a good job we know each other inside out! Besides there's only six months difference in age and it's always nice for me at the end of August, her birthday, to remind her that she is just that! She'll be twenty-six I remind myself in a few weeks, just after we return from Zante, oops I mean Zakynthos!

1 Airport hitch

One week later - mid August
Zante/Zakynthos

Ruby

We arrive on time at the international yet miniature airport. It's just after 4 am as I direct Adeline to the Departure Lounge - except there isn't a lounge as such, just a few rows of chairs, partitioned from the Arrivals Hall by a flimsy screen.

'Excuse me. Can I help at all?' a tour operator asks, as we plonk ourselves down in the plastic chairs. It sounds like she is from the Home Counties, and she's plastered in makeup even at this early hour.

'No thanks. We're just waiting here until daybreak,' I reply, sensing a battle is brewing already.

'The airport is closing now until the next flight arrives at 9am. You won't be able to stay in here,' she adds, clicking her blue court shoes as she continues to scowl down at us.

'Give us a few minutes and we'll be out of here. Before you go, what's the best resort for our age group on the island?'

She looks at me as if I'm asking for the Crown Jewels as she raises her eyebrows, and I notice the smudge of eyeliner under her right eye.

'Laganas is the resort for the 18-30's. But there's no bus till 9am. Here's a number for a taxi.' Turning on her heels, she ushers the dregs of the holidaymakers out to their waiting coaches.

'You'd think she could have let us on the coach,' huffs Adeline.

'I'd rather walk to be honest. That's my worst nightmare - being herded like cattle. I'll pay for a taxi. It's not your fault my bright idea has failed. Come on, let's get through Passport control.' I'm praying that they don't look at the back page of my passport. It's the first time back to Greece after the debacle with border control in Athens.

Hell! Too late, he's scrutinising the back page now, looking me up and down as if I'm a piece of meat that needs a good pummelling. Another official comes over to the desk, impatient to go home, but curious as to why his colleague is so interested in a tourist woman's passport. Adeline taps me on my arm.

'What's the matter Ruby. Has your passport expired?'

'No, it's ok. Just something in Greek on the back page. It'll be ok,' I hasten, praying they will let it go and allow us to stay on the island.

Eventually they point to the exit as they loosen their ties and take off their hats. A solitary taxi flashes its lights our way.
'But what about the phone number the stuffy tour rep gave us? Do you think this taxi is registered?' Adeline asks, with a slight tremble in her voice.

I don't answer as I urge her to keep up with my pace –I need to exit the airport before the customs official changes his mind and holds me back for questioning.

I'm also vexed that my plan has already gone awry, and the airport is shutting.

I kick myself for assuming that everything would go according to plan and for forgetting about the comments in my passport, written in Greek. I still haven't had them translated since fleeing from Athens a few years ago. I've been my own free spirit for so long now I guess I'm not used to thinking of others. I wonder how I come across to others? I make a mental note to myself to rein it in a bit. After all, it is my cousin's holiday too and she is used to the security of a package holiday with no dodgy goings on at Customs.

'Where you go ladies?'
'Erm, I forgot what resort she said now. Can you remember Adeline?' I ask as she shakes her head, suppressing a huge yawn.
'Oh, to hell with it, erm take us to where the young ones go, please?'

'You have room to stay?' the taxi driver asks, extinguishing a cigarette in his makeshift ashtray, stuck to the dash.
'No. We don't but if you take us to the busy resort, we can wait a few hours and find a hotel.' I instruct as we put our holdalls in the boot.

Half an hour later, the chain- smoking taxi driver with a faint scar across his right cheek stops outside the moderate sized Caretta Hotel, on what looks like the main road of the resort. I'm sure he's been taking us quite literally for a ride and driven round the same route a few times, but I'm in no mood for a confrontation.

At five in the morning the air is still but the silence is interrupted by the rustles of a few scrawny cats as they balance on the food skips, picking at leftovers. A middle-aged woman dressed in a white apron opens the shutters of a bakery. The mouth-watering aroma of fresh bread and pastry swirls towards us prompting us to breathe in deeply and be thankful we are actually here.

'This Caretta hotel is good price. You pay for week for the good price. They take you now,' the driver prompts. I shake my head. I remember a little bit of Greek from my three months in Athens as I instruct the driver to take us to the beach. I'm not committing to paying for a room when I don't even know where we are; and it doesn't look very lively either. It will all look better when daylight breaks, I assure myself. But for now, we can sit on the beach and watch the sun rise.

'It is not good to go on biich,' the driver snaps as I'm already opening the door of the boot to retrieve our bags.

'Don't worry mother, we'll be ok till morning,' I quip.

'Hey lady. You not go biich. It is the, erm – how I say in English?' He then reiterates in Greek 'Carretta, Carretta. You no go biich.' I figure he must be desperate to earn some commission from the

Caretta Hotel, so I feign ignorance and offer a wad of drachma notes. He throws some coins into my hand and then continues to return our bags into the boot. Adeline steps forward and retrieves them again, stepping on his foot as she does. He yelps out, hopping away and shouting some obscenities. I switch to my limited Greek again and urge him to drive away. He throws his arms in the air as a lit cigarette flies over our heads and lands in the dry shrubbery.

Eventually he screeches off, kicking up small stones with his wheels. I ask Adeline if she has a torch. She shakes her head. It's absolutely pitch-black as I just about make out the look of exasperation on her face. It's a look that could say - *and why would I have a torch? It's not something I tend to pack on a beach holiday!*

I half smile and wish we could fast forward a few hours to daylight. In the meantime, I need to regain my calmness and reassure my cousin that I am the confident 'nothing fazes me' world traveller that I portray. Fortunately, we have a great friendship as we both have no siblings and are more like sisters. At only six months apart in age, we've grown up together and even worn identical dresses that my mother made for us – some which we were relieved when we outgrew them.

I've tried with all my might to get her to come travelling with me, but she has a good career and is much more sensible and mature than me. And after this tricky start, I don't blame her if she continues with her package holidays. I might just join her next time if we struggle to find accommodation! Maybe my carefree travel days are naturally expiring?

I should have haggled more with the sleepy old lady at the Caretta Hotel! However, I can't be bothered to go back, and I gather from the stony reception they wouldn't want us to stay.

'Ruby, I can hear the waves.'

We hold on to each other as I tentatively check my footing on the embankment, which hopefully leads down to the beach.

I know we are both tired and disorientated but the fact that she can hear the waves spurs me on in the inky blackness. I wince as my ankle takes the brunt of the difference in levels as I step from the spiky embankment onto the soft sand.

'Here Addie, we're on the beach now but just be careful as you step on the sand. I take her hand as she throws her bag into the darkness, making a comforting thud as it lands on the sand. I did well to persuade her to pack the absolute minimal – it would have been much a nightmare with cumbersome suitcases!

'Here's some sunbeds. Let's lie on these until the sun comes up.'

Thankfully, Adeline slips quickly into a slumber, softly snoring with her beach towel tightly wrapped round her on the plastic sunbed. I can't get to sleep. I feel like her guardian angel as I survey our surroundings. Fuck! I think I can hear something. Something rustling and shuffling. My body is as stiff as a board. From the corner of my eye, I make out a low dark object which is no doubt a rat! Projectile vomiting threatens as I pray the shape passes Adeline and doesn't pick up her scent. Either she isn't giving off any aroma or the rat has better things to sniff as it scurries away in the undergrowth. I breathe again and hope there's not an entire family of them in tow.

A few minutes pass, as I edge my sunbed closer to Adeline's.
'Come on sunrise. Please, hurry,' I whisper as I will the waning moon to shoo off and allow the rising sun to take command of the skies. I check my watch and only minutes have elapsed since I last looked. Just what does it take for the dawn to make an

appearance here? I'm sure it gets lighter earlier back home. Adeline moans out in her sleep as she turns from side to side and the beach towel falls to the sand. I pick it up and wrap it around her again and sit on the bottom of her sunbed, wishing I could sleep too. But I'm the one responsible for this little pickle we're currently facing. What if there really are no budget hotels? What if we do have to resort to staying at the hotel the taxi driver was so intent on booking us into?

My eyelids need matchsticks to hold them up as another dark object brushes past, centimetres away and I cover my mouth to stifle a yelp. Then, my prayers are answered as I turn to the sea and a pale yellow ball ascends from the horizon. *'Thank you, thank you God for the sunrise. I owe you one.'*

'Ruby, Ruby. Where are we?'
'It's ok Adeline, don't worry. It's daylight now. Let's look for the main road and find a bus stop. This resort looks a bit too sleepy for two young

hedonists!' I need to keep a fast pace and keep my tone of voice confident.

We scramble up the side of the embankment again, but this time with the rising sun behind us and no beach rats in tow! It's strange how things look different in the light as I survey our surroundings and see wooden signs with roughly sketched pictures of turtles on the low walls surrounding the shrubbery. How we didn't fall over those last night I'll never know!

'Where do you think the bus stop will be?' Adeline asks scratching her head and scraping her blonde curls up in a bobble. She's very fair skinned and needs to be careful in the sun whereas I'm the opposite. Our mums are sisters and while Adeline's mum is as fair as they come, my mum could be mistaken for a southern Mediterranean with dark hair and olive skin. Grandad was Irish and Nan was English – a throwback in the gene-mixing pot. I'm pleased to have the darker gene though as I don't have the curse of the red onion peeling skin. Plus, I am happiest in the sunnier climes. I make a mental note to delve into our family history soon.

Any sign of a bus stop seems remote as Adeline swaps her holdall from one side of her shoulder to the other, while switching hands with the squeaky cassette player.
We amble along at the side of the road on the sandy pavement as the squeaking becomes like an annoying itch you can't quite get to as I offer to strap it to my holdall which is doubling as a backpack, strapped to my back.

The bleating of goats and the tinkling of bells in the near distance remind us of where we are as we carry on along the dust strewn road, feeling like extras in a Spaghetti Western. The sun is rising rapidly and bathing us with much needed warmth, forming swirls in the air. From out of nowhere, a small pickup truck abruptly brakes, kicking up small stones in its wake.

'Girls you need lift? Where you go?'

'We want to go to the busy resort,' I reply as Adeline shoots me a glance that I can't quite decipher.

'Girls, hop in the back. I go slowly. I take you to the Laganas. Very crazy there. You are there before?'

I shake my head at the eager Greek man as I position my hands around Adeline's backside and heave her into the back of the open pickup truck, littered with hessian sacks. A solitary black olive bounces around the metal base as we plonk ourselves down and the driver accelerates a little too hastily. The olive takes the path of the channels in the metal like a pinball machine, as Adeline yelps out.

'Jesus, get it off me!'

'It's only a butterfly.' I reassure her as she lifts her t-shirt up and down, revealing a little too much of her already tanned midriff. Oh Lordy, I hope she doesn't encounter any other critters that may inhabit this island. I suppose they don't bother me now, having just returned from *down under* – the land of arachnids, parasites and man-eating crocs.

'Girls. You ok in back?' the driver gives me a start as he emulates a dog with his head right out of the window, looking in the wrong direction. He swerves to avoid colliding with another pickup. A blast of horns ensues as he pulls himself back in his seat.

'Tell him to stop Ruby. I'll walk the rest of the way. This is friggin crazy.'

I'm about to bang on the window which separates the cab from the back as the driver applies the brakes and the olive returns to its starting point. He jumps out of the driver seat.

'Girls. You have room? If no. I have my cousin Spiro who has rooms at the start of the road to the beach. You will see the hotel. It is an Angel hotel.'

We thank him as we jump out of the pickup rather than waiting for him to drop the tailgate. I think the sooner I get a room sorted, the better. I didn't envisage so much drama at this early stage in the holiday. Although it's what I'm used to, I need to rein myself in and realise it's not the normal way to start a week's holiday on an idyllic Greek island. The pickup driver is already walking down the non-tarmacked road, gesticulating with a taller man with an elaborate spiral moustache. They stop talking as we approach and with a curt nod of his head, the pickup driver saunters back to his vehicle, turning his head back every so often.

It takes him some time to drive away as the tall thirtysomething man introduces himself.
'Kalimera girls. And my name is Spiro Angelos. My cousin Manolis says you no have room. I have room here in my hotel,' he says in a sing song voice as he sweeps his arm up in the air to alert us to the freshly painted *Angel Hotel* signage.
Adeline searches my face for approval. Although I would have usually had a good look round searching for the best room and deal, I realise as the hotel has

come with a recommendation and looks in good repair, we might as well relent and ask the price.

'I give you nice price for one week. Here I show the room. Please follow.'

Adeline looks delighted as the room is light and spacious with a wide balcony overlooking a modest size swimming pool and a view to the olive groves inland.

'Yes, this is good. How much please, *poso kani parakalo*?' I ask in Greek, in the hope that it will impress Spiro into giving us a good deal.

The amicable owner leaves us with a promise that he will have some fresh towels sent to the room as soon as possible. A quick glance into the bathroom suggests the previous guests, might have only just left.

'Ahh, this is nice. Thanks Ruby.'

'Hey, you don't have to thank me. I'm relieved it was a reasonable price and is clean, well except for the bathroom.' I haven't finished my sentence as she pads into the bathroom with her cassette player. Music is her life. Having graduated from the Manchester Royal College of Music, her heart is with her double bass which she plays professionally, when not in her day job at the bank. She loves all genres of music and probably can't wait till we hit the bars and music later. *I wonder if she'll love the authentic Greek music as I do?* I also hope we get the chance to take part in a more authentic Greek night too and throw a few plates over each other's heads! Suddenly, things are looking up.

Ten minutes later, having emptied our holdalls over the beds, we venture down the dirt road which must be the equivalent to the infamous Falaraki and Ayia Napa Strips. It seems like Laganas is just waking up to cater for the younger hedonists, as bar after bar advertise their Happy Hour times, careful not to coincide with each other. What is presently a dirt track leading down to the beach is fast being transformed into a proper tarmacked Strip with the ubiquitous tourist bars and semi- authentic tavernas. Something tells me we will have to travel elsewhere for a bouzouki night!

Although extremely tempting to have a swift cold beer, we head straight for the beach. The drinking can wait – well just for a few hours anyway. I can already imagine the amber liquid soothing my parched throat. Hell knows we deserve it! I also clocked the stands selling skewers of souvlaki. The aroma is seriously making my stomach rumble as I realise, we haven't eaten since the limp cheese and ham toastie on the plane.

2   Loving it in Laganas

Adeline

Having survived the airport fiasco, the altercation with the taxi driver and having no accommodation, I must admit I have quite enjoyed the adventure of the last twenty-four hours. Obviously, if we were still hauling our holdalls and my squeaky cassette player down the Strip, looking like a beleaguered Mary and Joseph in search of lodgings, it would be a different story. How my cousin lives her life just so free spirited and flighty always astounded me but now I've had the experience, I can understand her lifestyle more. And I must admit, I slept like a koala up a eucalyptus tree on that sun lounger - *maybe it's the way forward?* Goodbye to the package holiday and hello to living with a little less order and less punctilious planning.

I follow suit and step in line with Ruby as we plod along the sands looking for the best spot. There seems to be a distinct lack of younger holidaymakers right now as a few families gather round their beach towels, organising their day with snacks and sun lotion. A little boy tugs at his dad's hand, willing him to take him into the sea as he waits for instructions from the wife. They look Scandinavian with their blonde hair, toned bodies and designer beachwear. Then there's the typical juxtaposition of the British family, with Dad sporting his loose Union Jack swim shorts and mum slapping on hats and sunscreen as the kids wriggle around in the sand. I love people-watching, especially through my sunglasses. I just hope that I can be brave enough to venture into the sea again and enjoy its healing and soothing qualities, after the fool I made of myself last year on holiday when I mistook a pile of seaweed that had wrapped itself around me for an octopus! I must have looked pathetic, screeching the secluded bay down, sprinting out of the sea, trying to rip it off my legs. Then, to add insult to injury the day after, a jellyfish just happened to make a bee line for me. Fortunately, a drop dead gorgeous Spanish man came to my rescue, scooping me up in his brawny arms. Unfortunately, he plonked me down next to his drop-dead gorgeous girlfriend on the sand, while she squirted vinegar all over my legs.

Ruby returns from a quick dip in the sea, saying it's warmer than the sea in Cairns, as we both mould our weary bodies into the sand and try to think of absolutely nothing.

Cousins Manolis and Spiros

Manolis had been up since 3 am that morning when he spotted the two tourist girls walking on the main road from Kalamaki towards Laganas. He had been returning from the airport where he had spent four hours waiting for his order of rat traps to be released. Thus, upon seeing the two girls with their luggage, at such an early hour, he had no hesitation in stopping. After all, there was no harm in dropping them off at the start of the main road that led down to Laganas beach; he was passing there anyway on his way to the *Adults Only Spa* hotel in Keri, inland from the Keri lighthouse. Unfortunately, there was a prolific infestation on his beloved island of vermin, and although it kept him in business, he would rather not have his island becoming infamously known as *Rat* Island. He knew how important the new wave of tourists are to the economy of the island and equally aware of no matter how many olives, currants and citrus fruits grow in its rich soil, an island that has constantly battled with invaders cannot rely solely on its export produce alone to sustain its people. Moreover, the cultivation of the synonymous Zante currants that made their way to England, without paying excise duty to Venice, has also been a cause of disagreement in and already contentious history.

And now with the tourism boom, our island will become saturated.
Unfortunately, the exclusive resort had reported a few too many staff sightings of the dirty black rats

and had managed to control it without the guests being alerted. The manager had called him at 2 am, literally pleading with him to come as soon as possible, despite the ridiculous hour. Fortunately, his order had arrived from Athens as he had recently used all his stock due to the sheer demand and calls he had from the various establishments all over the island that were discovering the despicable rodents. It was ironic that although he didn't want his island infested, his pest control business he ran with his wife was booming.

He knew it was frowned upon to pick up young tourists these days but he was intrigued as to why they were walking down the main road at such an early hour with their luggage strapped to their backs. *Had they walked all the way from the airport*? He had a flashback of earlier that morning when he had driven past the airport and briefly glanced at similar tourists getting into Demetrius Pappas' taxi. How he loathed that man! If it were the same two girls, where had he dropped them off? Demetrius Pappas was his arch enemy and despite what had happened in the past, he felt no remorse for the lecherous one-time philandering kamaki!

When the tourists had started to flock to the island, mostly the fair skinned Northern Europeans, chasing the sun, Demetrius was caught on several occasions driving the new wave of tourists the long way round from the airport to their resort – doubling their fares. Only the previous year, he had been spotted curb crawling his way down the new strip, preying on the vulnerable inebriated females as they staggered out of the many bars in the early hours of the morning. What a despicable excuse of a man – the malaka wanker!

Thus, it was Manolis' duty to deliver the tourists safely to Laganas. He felt proud that by doing so he was upholding the reputation of his island's *philoxenia* – kindness to strangers. He was also thankful that he could deliver them to his cousin

Spiros's hotel at the start of the road that led down to the beach. It was becoming busier and busier with each tourist season - bars and clubs popping up, vying for attention with their garish neon signs. There were also rumours that the dirt road would soon be tarmacked. Apparently, the Northern European tourists were not used to having to dust themselves down from the inevitable dirt that would be flicked up at them each time a vehicle passed, especially the more affluent Germans and Scandinavians, who seemed to wear white clothing. He liked the tourists his island attracted, as although the British had the infamous drinking reputation, the Brits who visited Zante, were a little classier. A friend of a friend's son had worked the previous season in Malia, Crete and the stories that were relayed were enough to make the straightest of hair curl! And the young women were just as bad, if not worse than the young men as they paraded up and down the main strip wearing next to nothing. They would drink themselves into oblivion at the proliferation of bars, goaded on by their pals and onlookers as they competed with downing yards of beer, contained in huge glass vessels, ultimately spewing it all back up in the gutters!

He hoped for his island and its people, that the hedonistic behaviour would not reach Zakynthos. Only time would tell, he surmised.

Spiros Angelos

'Manoli, is that you my cousin? I have heard something about the two tourists you picked up,' he whispers into the phone, covering the mouthpiece.

'Spiro, what is it? Are they ok?' he replies as he sits down at the dining table in his humble cottage, that boasts the most enviable view of the Ionian Sea, close to the island's capital. His wife, Ariadne looks adoringly into her husband's eyes for clues, as she sets them down a plate of grilled fish and home-made fries. She has always wanted a potato fryer and since the passing of her mother, only now has she been brave enough to purchase one.

'They took a taxi with Demetrius,' Spiro adds as Manolis confirms he too saw them get into his taxi. He says goodbye to Spiro and sets down the phone.

'Manoli. What is it? Is it Spiro?'

'It is nothing my love. Spiro worries too much about his guests, you know how he worries unnecessarily,' he replies, bending the truth a little. After all, he doesn't want his wife to know he picked up two tourist girls, earlier in the morning. Maybe it was not such a good idea after all. Maybe times are changing on his island and the inherent *philoxenia,* is losing momentum. Unfortunately, what Spiro has just relayed to him about Demetrius and the two tourists, means that he could be dragged into it if anything happened to them. If anything untoward were to follow, he is adamant that his dear wife will be protected. He loves his wife dearly and although he too has played the kamaki – *he who hunts with a spear,* in his youth, when the first influx of hippie females arrived on his island, he certainly didn't want his good reputation to be tainted. He must admit, he did have fond memories of that era and fortunately any rumours of his promiscuity down in Zante town, failed to travel up to his village.

Meanwhile, Spiros deliberates what to do for the best. He eventually reasons with himself, over a frappe, as he sits at the bar of his hotel, that it would be best to move the two English girls to the basement room; he hopes they won't be too disappointed and if they are he could soften the blow by offering them a free meal each day, for the remainder of their stay. His main priority is to keep them safe. If he was to be honest with himself, he finds them a little different from the other young women who party in Laganas. They exude a certain warmth and honesty. And the enigmatic young woman with the dark hair and striking blue eyes also knows a little Greek. She also seems familiar but he can't just put his finger on it. The fairer skinned girl with the blonde curly hair and angular features informed him they were cousins and are having a cheap break away from the rain in Manchester. He shakes his head as if it will jog his memory to remember which names belong to which woman – Ruby and Adeline, both pretty names he thinks. The niggling feeling doesn't go away as Spiro sorts out the bills from last night's bar takings until they return to the hotel. It's also time to keep his eyes on Walter, his Danish barman, whom seems to be attracting the attention of the young women who sunbathe topless around his pool. And although he hasn't been an angel himself and is certainly not a prude, he also wishes they would cover up, leaving more to the imagination. Maybe it's his strict upbringing or maybe just getting older, surmises.

Adeline and Ruby
As the girls make their way back from the beach, intent on eyeing up the various bars they might visit that evening, they don't notice the Greek eyes upon them from the various eateries and souvenir shops.

Word has reached Laganas about the two tourists who slept on the beach down at Kalamaki. Half the watchful eyes intend to keep them safe, the other half intend to teach them a lesson.

Depending on how many collaborate with each other will determine whether the Zante police should be informed. Little do they realise that the taxi driver, Demetrius has already been to the police and lodged a formal complaint.

'Do you fancy a swift beer here?' asks Ruby as they pass Zeus bar where a lone bartender, sporting an oversize baseball cap, arranges the glasses like soldiers in neat rows.

'If you don't mind I'd like to freshen up first. The sand plays havoc with my skin. And I'm itching to sit on that wraparound balcony looking over the pool. Actually, why don't we buy some cans of beer at this shop? Surely Spiros won't mind,' Adeline replies as her cousin swiftly swings round to enter the Minimart.

After tittering a little at the Greek God and his erect penis keyring, they pay for the cans and a couple of bags of nuts and make their way back to the Angel Hotel.

'Girls. Welcome back to the hotel. I need to speak with you. Please come into the reception office,' Spiro urges as soon as they enter the grounds.

'What is it Spiro? Have we done something wrong?' asks Ruby, opening two beer cans and offering one to Adeline.

'No, no, girls. I need a, how you say? I need a favour from you,' Spiros continues, slumping a little in his worn leather swivel chair.

Adeline's eyes widen as she splutters into her can.

'Girls I am so sorry but I have made a double booking. I need your room back for some other guests that have paid many months ago. I can offer you another room down below. It is the same size and with your price you have already paid, I will cook you a meal each night with free drinks for half of an hour. Please accept my mistake.' Spiros lights a cigarette, offering one to the girls as he waits for their response. He struggles to understand their quick conversation, shuffling a pile of paperwork around on his desk, hoping they will understand his dilemma.

'Well we are disappointed but we will stay for one night and see how we go on,' Adeline replies, taking the lead as she takes another swig from the can.

Collecting their clothes from the bed that they have not even had chance to hang up, they follow Spiros as he leads them down the marble steps to the basement room.

'Please girls I will make you the best Greek food tonight at 8pm in the bar area and I will send down some fresh towels.' The offer of food must have swayed it for them, as the damp room he stores the garden equipment in during the winter, is substandard to say the least. If the police come snooping, they will not think to look in the basement.

In the meantime, he will offer his barman a few extra free meals if he keeps close tabs on the girls and follows their every move; Demetrius Pappas must not know where they are! If Demetrius is aware that Manolis stopped and gave the girls a lift to Laganas, from wherever he had dumped them, he will endanger them, that's for sure – if his memory does not fail him.

Adeline

I wonder what my two friends, Nancy and Lorraine would make of this holiday scenario! One thing I have learnt from it in the brief time we have been here is it really is ok to be spontaneous and flexible. That's why I spoke up before my cousin and accepted the basement. After all, it's no one's fault and I guess it will be ok for a couple of nights before we find something else. I do miss the balcony though – the reason for me bringing my cassette player is so I can play some tunes while getting ready for the night out. As I'm always the first ready when I go away with Nancy and Lorraine, I take my wine, sit on the balcony and listen to a bit of Luther Vandross. But I suppose the sun won't wake us up in the morning from our ground level as I spot the only window, which is level with the pavement above.

Ruby

Fuck! I thought it was all going a little too well. It's not the fact that we've had to move rooms, as I'm determined to find us another hotel, it's more the fact that I feel like we are being followed. It's that unnerving feeling I've had before when I've been in less touristy places such as the war- torn countries in Central America -the hollow stares from the locals, weighing you up and down, wondering if you have come to cause trouble.

However, this is an idyllic Greek island but that sixth sense just won't subside. I truly wish I'd insisted on accommodation now when Davey at the travel agent sold us the flights. Now I know when he winked at his female colleague, the cheeky get. I'll have a word with him when we get back.

Oh well, one thing for sure is that we won't be spending any more time than needs be in this depressing room. I can't wait to get out and have a few or more beers. I'm hoping the alcohol will settle my nerves. While I wait for the bathroom, I select a Madonna cassette and slip it into the player as I fast forward to *Get into the Groove* - if Madge fails to get us in a party mood, I don't know who or what will.

Spiros

Walter my bartender has agreed to follow the girls around Laganas and phone me immediately if he sees anyone acting suspiciously. I think I can rely on him. After all he's confirmed that the girls haven't been down to the bar area as yet, so he should blend in with the other blond boys, seeking out the attention of a tourist girl. Although, I have warned him not to make sexy time with either of them! That would hinder their safety and my plan – whatever my plan is. Manolis also thinks that Demetrius remembers more than he lets on and is hell bent on revenge.

Thus, it is our duty to protect the women. Also, I must ask what exactly happened all those years ago between them. My cousin Manolis is eight years my senior and it was when he and his friend were babysitting me when I was a child as I could not get to sleep and heard them speak in hushed tones. That was the first time I felt my blood stop in my veins as I peered out through my bedroom keyhole and saw the shape of a kitchen knife being handed over as the moonlight shone into the hallway. Surely if he thinks the girls are in danger, he will now reveal the truth.

Walter

I'm so glad I did the reverse of what my parents wanted me to do for my gap year from my studies– *go to America and volunteer in a youth camp, they said – it will look good on your resume*! No way did I want to spend my precious time yelling at someone else's brats for the summer so I told mother and father a few hours before the flight to Zante departed. Obviously, they were shocked and annoyed but so be it, as I'm now doing what I want to do. Besides, you're only young once and all that jazz. And so far, so good. I've a great job at the Angel Hotel working as bar manager even though there's only the two of us. Plus, I have been asked by Spiros to keep an eye out on a couple of English beauties who are staying in the basement. Apparently, he's worried about them, so I must follow them around and make sure they are safe. Spiros has even given me drinking money!

I dress head to toe in black, trying to look inconspicuous but my blond hair stands out. When I make the mistake of popping into the Minimart to buy a black baseball cap, I'm stuck there with the older lady, Maria. She holds onto my arm and refuses to let go until I have repeated a few Greek phrases.

Figuring I'm a hopeless student and not in the mood to learn her phrases, as I have a feeling she is teaching me some profanities, she eyes me up and down, prodding my ribs and squeezing my thighs. It starts to tickle as I can't suppress my laughter and she roars like a lion. Her ample bosom jiggles up and down as the motion mesmerises me and I can't tear my eyes away. Maria scuttles off, her hips sashaying, into the back room as I'm just about to make my exit. She returns with various pastries, stuffing them into my hands and telling me to *tro tro* – eat eat. For some reason, I bow down to her as if she's royalty then leg it out, remembering I need to keep the girls in my vision.

What a shit bodyguard I am! I've failed already. I can't see them anywhere. Spiros will no doubt sack me off the job and demote me – probably to cleaning the toilets and hell that's not a job I would ever want to do – especially here in Greece where we have to throw the used toilet paper into the open basket. I remember the first day I experienced it – I nearly spewed my guts up on the yellowed walls. I'm sprinting now, looking like a clown who's lost the circus as I scan the myriads of tourists milling around the souvenir shops and bars. I trip myself up as the thin rubber detaches itself from my cheap flip flops and I land with an almighty thud on the hard earth. A throng of scantily dressed females come to my rescue as I'm swiftly hauled onto a soft bucket seat at the front of a bar.

'Hey, are you the barman from the Angel Hotel?' asks the blonde girl, who I'm supposed to be following. She removes my cap and checks my head for any bleeding. I nod and wince as her fingers find the bump that's popping up on my skull. The proximity of her arm pit and the musky scent, send my senses into overdrive as in a fleeting moment I imagine myself in bed with her. The other girl, her cousin, Spiros informed me, fetches something from the bar. My eyes are heavy as she parts my lips and feeds me some sort of amber spirit which burns yet soothes my throat. Then, they're gone again. Shit, I mumble under my breath as the handsome pharmacist who I've had my eye on for a while rushes over the road and takes my temperature as I smile into his deep brown eyes. After a few minutes rest , the handsome pharmacist, whose name badge reveals is *Theo*, gives me the thumbs up as I dash out in hot pursuit of the girls. The only problem now is that I've blown my cover, and they know who I am. Do I tell Spiros, or do I just go along with it? Besides, I can always pretend I'm taking a few days off from the bar and hope they allow me tag along with them. And they do look like fun. There's something that sets them apart from the other tourists.

Laganas beach 2pm

'Hey Ruby, there's that lad again. That one there, on the pink towel.' Ruby lifts her head slightly, tips her sunglasses and confirms it's the blond lad from the hotel bar.

'He's a bit of all right him, isn't he Addie? I could see you two together – two blond beauties in paradise. '

'And his accent is sexy as. I reckon Dutch or Scandinavian!' remarks Adeline as she rearranges her bikini bottoms. 'I'm going to keep an eye on him anyway. It looks like he's asleep and I'm sure you should stay awake after a bump to the head.'

'Nurse Adeline to the rescue,' Ruby adds as she makes a heart shape with her fingers.

The beach is alive with laughter as giddy children chase each other into the sea, while others concentrate on making the biggest sandcastles they have ever built. A thin local man with bandy legs strolls up and down selling a variety of fruit in bags as their juices drip out through the soggy paper.

The atmosphere is sublime as Adeline changes the Luther cassette to a Bob Marley tune, turning the volume to a desirable level so as not annoy other sunbathers. She lies down, keeping the blond boy in her peripheral vision.

Unbeknown to Adeline, Walter is doing the same under his shades. Soon he will have to execute plan B – to gain the sympathy of the girls so they invite him to tag along with them.

He nearly drifts off as mini people with mini hammers bang tiny nails into his skull. If it persists, he might have to seek out the pharmacist guy again! Yet, he also likes what he can see right in front of him as Adeline turns to lie on her front, leaving her fine derriere on show. It sure is a tricky, being bi-sexual, he muses or is it *the best of both worlds*?

2.30pm Laganas beach

'Right, that's it. I'm going over to him. He hasn't moved a muscle for half an hour.' Ruby doesn't answer her cousin as she too is asleep.

'Hello, hello there. Are you ok? We helped you after your fall. And we're a bit concerned as you need to stay awake following a bump to the head.' Adeline kneels on his beach towel, her bikini clad body inches away from his face.

'Oh! Shit, shit! Did I fall asleep? I'm so sorry, ermm,'

'Adeline. My name's Adeline. Do you remember me and my cousin? You remember, after your fall?'

She kneels down fully and takes off his baseball cap, inspecting the glowing red bump as Walter's face meets her breasts. Regaining a little composure he replies.

'Adeline. I'm sorry you have been worried. I think I am ok. Just a little sleepy,' Walter answers, glad the pretty blonde, with the chocolate brown eyes, has made the first move.

Enter Plan B - hopefully without Spiro finding out that he blew his cover, within the first hour.

The only flaw with Plan B, Walter worries about, is tagging along with the two beauties, night and day, unless he displays he's interested in the delicious

Adeline - which would not be a complete charade anyway, as she finally stands up as he feels something stirring in his groin that he hasn't felt for a long time in the presence of a female. Things are beginning to look up!

Adeline

Oh, sweet Jesus, I think I'm in love! But how can I be when I've only just met him? This is insane but I'm not going to deny that as soon as I knelt next to him, my heart raced along with something else between my legs! I've not even been bothered with men since my dirty rat of a boyfriend cheated on me with a much older woman, a MILF, I think they call them, exactly one year ago this week. When I confronted him, he relayed he liked his women to make an effort in the lingerie and make up department, and she ticked all his boxes. Well there was no way I was going to switch from my M&S comfortable knicks and bras just for a shallow dick like him!

Anyway, he's history and this blond boy is ticking all my boxes with the bonus he's Dutch, Danish or Scandinavian.

Ruby

I wake from a weirder than usual daydream as I spot Adeline frolicking about in the sea with the bartender who smelt divine when we nursed his bump, just a few hours ago. I prop myself up on my elbows and take a swig of warm water. It's good to see her in the sea as she's not usually at ease in the water and although she can swim, she still has bad memories from a prank that got out of hand in her local swimming baths.

I'm so glad I orchestrated this whole holiday. I can't really afford it but it was a ruse to show her how she can and will get over that dickhead, Nigel Cockshot, whom I don't know but if I hadn't have been on the other side of the world, I would not have hesitated to shoot a slingshot right at his pathetic excuse of a cock! Anyway, that's history and my cousin and I are having a wonderful time, despite the rocky start here on this little jewel in the Ionian Sea. Even the slightly unnerving feeling that someone is watching us isn't spoiling the cathartic effect of being back on a Greek island.

I have an urge to join them in the sea, but I leave them to it as I'm getting the distinct feeling that this blond boy quite likes my cousin and vice versa! If he doesn't tag along too much it's just what I wanted to happen as I hear my cousin giggle with her shapely legs wrapped around his slim waist.

Playing a big ripe gooseberry to the two blondies suddenly seems inevitable now!

'Ruby. This is Walter from Rotterdam. Walter this is my best friend and cousin Ruby.'

I shake his hand and tell him *I love him,* in Dutch, instead of saying, *how are you.* His bright blue eyes twinkle in confusion as he scratches his head. Suddenly, it's my turn for a dip in the sea.

The iridescent water soothes my feet as I plunge into its warmth and lie on my back, allowing my face to feel the harsh heat of the sun for just a few minutes. Mum always gives me a lecture on safety in the sun each time I go away, sneaking in the highest factor sunscreen into my bag, which I pretend to use.

I return to the love birds as I notice Walter's pink beach towels next to Adeline's. Inches separate them as their fingers intertwine. I stand over them and check they are both sleeping. Adjusting the parasol to cover their faces, I pick up my bum bag, tucking Adeline's under the towel close to her, as I slink away.

The beach is a long, crescent moon bay, with only a handful of low rise hotels and eating establishments, dotted along the edge, where sand meets gravel. The most delicious aromas waft towards me in the sea breeze, as my tummy moans and groans. After my short stroll, I'll suggest we go for food. I saunter in and out of the gently lapping waves knowing how rich in minerals it is; I can feel the beneficial qualities already, infiltrating my pores. A large sign at the far end of the beach catches my attention as I lift my sunglasses.

It reads: *Warning! It is prohibited to enter the beach from the hours of 2100 - 0700 May to September on the beaches around Laganas and Kalamaki Bay. Here is where the famous Caretta Caretta Loggerhead turtles nest and hatch. Fines in place….*

I don't read any further, as my heart beats like a fist against my ribcage and my knees buckle beneath me as I slump to the sand in an exaggerated movie clip. 'Fuck! How stupid am I? I mutter under my breath as a couple of young lads, sporting knotted hankies to their heads, approach. They've seen my fall from grace as they stop mid- march.

'Hey love. Are you ok?' they enquire in unison as they offer their hands and ease me up to a sitting position.

'Yeah, I just tripped up I think,' I assure them, patting down my sarong and wishing the sand would swallow me up.

'Ok love. As long as you're sure. I'm Lee and this is my twin Ryan. Pleased to meet you. You sound like a fellow Manc. Are you from Manchester?'

'Yes, I sure am. And thanks for your help and I thought I was seeing double then!' I reply, eager to brush them off as quickly as I can, but without seeming rude.

'Ahh yeah. We get a lot of that. Maybe because we look identical,' Lee says as they both chortle and dig each other playfully in the arm. I roll my eyes at them and wish them a good holiday as they continue on their 'tit patrol.' I follow them with my eyes as they periodically nod to each other and I realise, for the first time since being on the beach, the abundant display of bare breasts.

I'm drawn to a nearby beach bar where a few Union Jack flags are draped from the ceiling, along with a plethora of bikinis, bras and thongs, waiting patiently for their owners to collect them.

My first beer doesn't even touch the sides as the bartender raises his eyebrows and nods his head for confirmation that I need another one. The second goes down slightly slower as I deliberate if I should tell Adeline about the turtles.

'Excuse me. Is that Kalamaki beach?' I ask the bartender, pointing in the direction of the other side of the bay.

'Yes it is. Why? Are you staying there? Do you need to know if you can walk from here? The answer is yes. But please be careful of our *chelona* – the turtle.' He gives me an enquiring nod as he leaves to serve some more customers.

Hell, now it all makes sense. Now I understand why the enraged taxi driver was adamant that we should not go down to the beach. Those poor, poor turtles!

What if we have inadvertently endangered the baby turtles that might have just been ready to hatch from their shells and make their first tentative paddle down to the sea? What if we even trod on some and killed them so soon into their new life? I actually hate myself for being so dumb and playing the *'worldly wise traveller'*

Shit. Maybe the taxi driver informed the police! Maybe that's why I have felt like someone is following us especially that ubiquitous policeman who we keep bumping into. Oh hell, Ruby, Ruby, Ruby what a tit you are!

I pay for my two large beers and decide to return to Adeline and Walter. I'll either stay silent about the turtle revelation or spurt it out in my haste to unburden my heavy heart and conscience.

Laganas Strip - later that night

Laganas is bouncing as a river of hedonistic youths, ascend on the main drag as if they've been let loose from boarding school, intent on making up for lost time. They congregate in groups as they deliberate on which bar is offering the best deals on cocktails and shots. Tonight, they are on holiday without a parent in sight. Tonight they are free to do whatever they damn well like. Although the island is in its early stages of opening up to the younger tourists, word has spread like wildfire and this August has seen the most tourist footfall ever, through its small international airport.

At the rate it is growing, it might have to stay open all night and employ more staff.

Most islanders are comfortable with the sudden increase in tourism, others not so. The inhabitants living in the villages in the interior of the island are mostly oblivious as to the shenanigans that go on in Laganas, down on the coast. What's more, they will probably never visit the resort as long as they live. There are a handle of the older generation, however, who genuinely enjoy the tales of crazy Northern

Europeans drinking themselves to oblivion, spewing up and having sex on the beach. They remember the dark years of the dreadful Civil War. The deadened sadness in their neighbours' eyes; the wailing of villagers as they were informed their sons and husbands had been slaughtered; the shortage of basic foods where the island was its own fortress. To commemorate the fallen, the Kambi Cross stands tall and proud on a promontory close to the cliffs, the grey cement, reflecting the dull hearts of the loved ones of the fallen. A stark reminder, the huge cross can be seen many miles out at sea.

Thus, the Zakynthians are now content to welcome a new wave of invader – the visitors who bring fun, laughter and cash. And if they don't descend on their villages and run riot nor endanger their precious Carreta Caretta chelona turtle around the island's shores, they are most welcome.

That evening, Ruby and Adeline have one of the best nights of their lives. Ruby restrained from imparting the information on the notice board, but she figures Adeline may already be aware as Walter is a wealth of information on Zante. He's not come up for air since the three of them sauntered back to the hotel from the beach as they stopped at the stall to sample the souvlaki sticks. Unbelievably, they also made it back to the hotel without being tempted into one of the bars, lining the un-tarmacked main drag.

'I'm having the best night of my life,' yells Adeline as she throws her arms up in the air and twirls around the makeshift dancefloor of Zero's bar. A trained ballerina as well as musician, the dance floor is her stage as she half pirouettes, half break dances to the beat of Shaggy's ,Mr Boombastic, followed by Salt n' Pepa's, Push It. Walter just can't restrain himself either as he joins her on the floor with a Dutch version of how *not* to dance! Ruby observes from her safe distance, genuinely pleased for her cousin as the English rose and the Flying Dutchman take hold of each other, fitting neatly together like a jigsaw. A holiday romance is just what she needs to boost her ailing confidence after dickhead Cockshot did the dirty! Ruby muses as her mind wanders to Denny, the lad from Warrington she met in Australia and whether anything will come of it when they get back home. Her thoughts are momentarily broken as a Rugby team take over the dance floor with a rendition of 'Swing low, sweet chariot 'as a great brawny brute sweeps her off her feet and holds her above his head, twirling her round in circles as the kaleidoscopic lights follow her in a frenzied game of catch up.

The feeling of his secure muscular arms and a hint of aftershave sends her head swirling with a lustful longing for him to be hers for the night. A one night stand with no strings attached.

As Adeline and Walter retreat with the hotel door key, Ruby reassures them that she's in safe hands and won't be coming back for at least an hour as

Bryn the rugby player suggests they clear their heads outside.

'No. We can't go on the beach. It's protected for the turtles,' Ruby explains as she slips her arm into Bryn's.

'Nah. It'll be ok. We were on the beach in the sea at 2 am last night,' he responds, looking down at her petite 5'3" frame from his 6'3" height.

'Well you shouldn't have been on the beach at all. And what do you mean 'we'? Another female, I imagine. Actually Bryn, thanks for the dance and all that but I'm going back to the hotel. I'm knackered anyway – it's been an eventful day!'

Ruby doesn't wait for a response as she sways up the main strip, ignoring the salacious advances from a few groups of lads as she joins Spiro at the bar at the Hotel Angel.

Spiro

'You are alone Ruby. And why is this?' asks Spiro as he helps her up to the bar stool and thrusts a glass of water into her hand.

'Oh I'm ok Spiro. My cousin is having a little sexy time with Walter so I thought I would come and keep you company.'

'With Walter! You mean the Walter who works here in the bar? Pah! Useless malaka!'

'No, no Spiro. He is useful actually. He is making my cousin smile again.'

Enraged that Walter had let him down by giving away his identity, he decides to ask the inebriated Ruby to relay the events from when they first arrived at the airport to warrant his concern for their safety.

'I need a brandy first please.' As Spiro mixed an ample amount of lemonade to the Greek brandy, Ruby settles on the stool and inhales deeply.

'Ok. I guess I was just used to being responsible for just one person and that person was just me. How was I to know that the bloody airport would shut? I mean, come on. Have you ever known such a bizarre thing as an airport shutting up for the night? Anyway, well where was I? Ah, yes so there we were, me and my cousin Addie. with just holdalls to carry. No suitcases just holdalls. Oh, and a bloody squeaky cassette player. Anyway, so then this stuck-up bitch of a tour rep – oh from the Home Counties, don't you know. Well, she...'

'I am sorry Ruby but please I do not follow well. Please tell me without all this detail. Just facts about the taxi please,' Spiro interjects, wondering if he should have waited till morning to ask a less inebriated Ruby, when her head was clearer.

'Ah. Sorry Spiro. Ok well, yes like I was saying, this bitch told us to hop it out of the airport and well err, oh and then there was a problem with my passport. Oh Spiro. Tomorrow, I will show you my passport and you translate the Greek words for me. I need to know now and then well ....' Ruby's head falls forward as Spiro leaps over the bar to catch her mid fall. Taking all her drunken weight, he carries her in his arms down to the basement as she snores gently in his arms, with a strange but beautiful face. Oh, if only he was fifteen or so years younger, he dreams as he navigates the marble steps with caution.

'What the hell!' exclaims Adeline as she searches for her towel that has fallen off the single bed. Walter leaps off Adeline, tanned buttocks on show, as he falls with a thud to the hard flagged floor.
'Walter! I do not pay you to make sexy time with my guests. Pack your bags and out of my hotel.'
Spiro's veins are bulging and pulsating like the Incredible Hulk, a time bomb, as he throws Walter's clothes up the marble stairs.

'I am sorry about my bartender. I told him to keep watch for you as I worry about the taxi driver and then he takes my piss and makes sexy time with you. I thought Walter had an eye for the boys, but now not. I don't understand the youth today. I go and look for another barman or maybe I employ a woman.' Spiro makes eye contact with Ruby before he too takes the marble steps to his seat behind reception.

3 Making waves in Kalamaki

Walter   6am the following morning
I always go with my gut feeling and although I will miss the lovely ballerina Adeline and this amazing view from my room, fate has played the joker card and it is now time to leave. Travel to pastures new, before I become complacent and let my heart rule my head.
Plenty more opportunities and plenty more fish in the sea -, so they say.
I watch my last sunrise from the rooftop which I have had the pleasure of the penthouse room for the last six months, write a quick note for Adeline, take the

steps down to the dingy basement and push it under her door.

The sun is climbing higher as I gather my pace up the dusty road with my backpack on my back, like a character from the film, *Once Upon a time in Mexico* as stumpy palm trees, juxtaposed with tall Cypress trees, wave me on my way. The aroma of wild hillside herbs revitalises my senses as I nod my head and say my farewells to Laganas – it's been a pleasure and a blast. I make it just in time to hop on the first bus of the day to the airport.

Spiro and Manolis

'Manoli. I have been trying to contact you all morning. My barman blew his cover on the first night and then took advantage of one of the girls. I found them in bed together. Pah, I must admit I was jealous. I miss my wife, Manoli . She was too young to leave us.

'Spiro. I am sorry but I have been crazy busy with the vermin that are taking over our island. And I only can imagine how heartbroken and lonely you must be my dear cousin. And that is disgusting about the barman, Pah, the Dutch malaka. What news do you have?'

'I have spoken to the girls again this morning about the taxi ride and I do not feel we need to have them followed all the time now. It is very unlikely they will leave Laganas, as they are doing what the Northern European tourists do. They have found their comfort zone in Laganas and they will party at night and sleep in the day. I have been watching the ways of these tourists for two years since I bought the hotel, and their holiday habits and rituals are like clockwork. Please my cousin, do not worry and try to make peace with yourself and rid your unhealthy thought s of Demetrius. It will only be you who suffers, not him,' Spiro whispers into his phone, behind his small reception where he is still sat from the previous evening, only leaving his post to go to the toilet a few times.

'Cousin, for once in your life, you make sense. I think it is also now time to let bygones be bygones and although Demetrius is the reason I have no children, I will thank the Lord I have my beautiful wife. Thank you, my cousin. I will stop by soon. But first I need to rid our paradise from the vermin. Has there been any sighting of them in Laganas do you know Spiro?' Manolis stubs his cigarette in the ashtray in the cab of his pickup as he reaches for his worry beads, hanging from the rear-view mirror – he needs to keep his fingers busy all the time, a trait of his nervous disposition.

'Vermin is vermin. They are everywhere Manoli. But I have not heard any news that there is an infestation here in Laganas. But of course, I will keep both ears open and contact you at once. You do an excellent job cousin. Bye for now.' Spiro twiddles the flex of the green telephone around his fingers; one of a few habits he has picked up having given up smoking two years ago when his beautiful wife passed away with lung cancer. To Spiro, Elpida, is irreplaceable and will be in his heart forever. Even the scantily clad tourist females who frolic around in his pool with their bare breasts bobbing and sploshing up and down, fail to stir any sexual desire in him.

Ruby is another matter though! She even looks Greek, with her olive skin and dark wavy hair. *Could she be the woman to restore his libido? Could she heal his shattered heart and psyche?* But she is also a tourist from a different country and culture, and that might be a bad combination.

Adeline

I can't believe what I'm reading. A note pushed through our basement room door informs me that Walter, the man that I have so quickly fallen for, has now left my life as swiftly as he entered it. I try to feign nonchalance, but my cousin knows me far too well to know that I'm devastated. We sit at the poolside bar, pushing our breakfasts around our plates as Spiro asks us if we know anyone who wants a bar job.

'Do you know where Walter went?' I ask him as he twirls the ends of his thin moustache around his fingers.

'He said it was time to go,' Spiro replies as he takes the pool net and skims the surface of the highly chlorinated water.

'Ruby, what do you think of taking off for a few days somewhere else on the island?' I ask, desperate to leave Laganas and the memory of the flying Dutch man who will be in the air right now unless he has ventured to another area of the island. So much has happened in just a few days as I yearn for him to come back to me, but I know that's not going to happen. Obviously, I felt more about him than he did me. I manage to eat a piece of feta cheese and bread and take a slurp of coffee as Ruby excuses herself to go to the loo. I look up to see Spiro approach the bar area. He pours himself a coffee, adding two heaped teaspoons of sugar and sits next to me. He says nothing until Ruby reappears.

'Girls. I need to explain. I worry about you girls from when you first arrive, so I ask Walter to follow you to keep you safe. When I see him making sexy time with Adeline, I feel betrayed, so I tell him to leave and now I deeply regret it. The Dutch man makes the best *'slow comfortable screw against the wall'* in all of the Laganas. I wish now I did not tell him to leave.' Spiro stares at his Greek coffee as though the grains are formulating an answer and then takes his worry beads out from a drawer and vigorously clacks them around his fingers.

I'm annoyed at Spiro. If it wasn't for him being so paranoid about thinking we are in danger, he would never have found us in bed together and Walter would still be with me. Thus, that's why we need to leave. We've had a crazy night out now, so I think it is time to move on too. I feel like I want to explore this beautiful island. I really fancy exploring the interior and the rustic, red roofed villages that are no doubt, a world away from these coastal resorts.

As the day turns into dusk, we accept the home cooked meal from Spiro. He takes us up to the rooftop patio where a pristine laid table awaits us. As we take our seats, the lady from the MiniMart, who on our first visit, grinned with us as she wrapped up our penis keyring in blue and white paper, expertly climbs up the fire escape stairs, her plump arms laden with a tea towel covered basket.

Ahh! Ta koritsia mou, my girls, troo, troo, eat, eat,' she urges as she puts her fingers to her mouth and sets the dishes in front of us. Shiny stuffed vine leaves, oven baked potatoes and a whole sea bream wait to be devoured. She stays to debone the fish, much to our relief as a glass eye looks up at us from the silver platter.

While we eat, Spiro reiterates how sorry he is about Walter as we inform him we are moving on anyway. He leaves us to drink in the sunset as the bold red sun sinks into the glistening waters, returning to refill our wine glasses a few too many times before we insist, we have had enough.

'Girls. I want you to stay. I want you to stay in the penthouse room here on the rooftop for the rest of your holiday.

The eagerness in his eyes is that of redemption. I speak for my cousin as she swirls the dregs of the local wine around in her glass.

'Spiro. Thank you for your kind offer but our minds are made up. We want to explore more of your wonderful island.'

I tell Ruby that I can't keep my eyes open. She seems in the mood for another night down the Strip - I suggest she asks Spiro to accompany her.

'I've seen the way he lusts for you. He just can't take his chocolate brown eyes off you,' I add as she smirks and throws me a V sign.

Spiros and Ruby

I make sure Adeline is softly snoring into her pillow before I take a quick shower and slip on a cool cotton shift dress. Adeline assures me she will be fine as long as I lock the door, and I take a pair of her new M&S knickers out of the 3 pack. Quite what she in implying, I will never know but in hindsight, I wish I had followed her advice on that bikini wax!

My next dilemma is how to wear my hair – up or down?

I settle on an up do as I gather my curls in a scrunchie, allowing a few strands to break free then twirl them round in my finger and let them dangle by the side of my sun kissed face.

My hands shake a little as I anticipate the sound of Spiros' husky voice. I also wonder how he scrubs up as blow an air kiss to the sleeping Adeline and close the door softly behind me.

Spiros meets me at the reception as I climb the marble steps and catch him looking at his reflection in the small, mottled mirror, perched precariously on a narrow shelf. He looks a little too formal in a white long-sleeved shirt, dark trousers.

'Ruby. I think my feet are like a tourist. I do not wear flip flops but tonight I think it is good. And Ruby, you are beautiful,' he adds, almost as an afterthought, as he kisses me on my lips and my head spins like a tumble dryer.

After a few cocktails in a cosy bar tucked away on the other side of the beach front, Spiro takes my hand and leads me to the hypnotic sound of the sea.

'But Spiro, we shouldn't be on the beach at night because of the chelona turtles. I read about it on the boards on the beach.'

'Ruby, I am an islander, and the signs are there to stop the tourist parties on the beach. A couple taking an evening swim is perfectly acceptable. Here, please. We take our clothes off and leave them under the sunbed.' Spiro senses my reluctance as I shuffle my feet in the sand.

'Ok we will walk further away so no one can see us. Let us take a walk to Kalamaki. It will be good for you to return and make your peace with the beach.'

A reluctant smile spreads across my face as I feel like a little girl not knowing how to respond – knowing that we are doing wrong but for all the right reasons – revisiting the beach where we potentially endangered the hatchlings will ease my conscience.

Halfway along the beach to where Laganas meets Kalamaki beach, Spiro stops and turns me to face the sea. Feeling his urgency, I follow him as we stride toward the choppy water. Whispering as quietly as possible, Spiro explains that it's quite a phenomenon that at this time of night and only for a few hours, the sea is perturbed, an angry being, as it gurgles and groans and hisses and growls. A few minutes go by as it retreats into its cage to usual state of calmness. Likewise, the phenomenon has affected the gentlemanly Spiro as I hear him groan. He reaches out to me and takes me to his bare chest and hardness.

'Ruby. I think the Goddess is at work.'

'What do you mean?' I ask as I instinctively wrap my legs around his waist, and we work our bodies against the force of the waves.

'It is the Goddess Aphrodite at play. In our language, *Aphros* means foam and the Goddess Aphrodite was born from the white foam produced by the severed genitals of Uranus, the God of Heaven when Cronos, his son, threw him into the sea!'

Maybe it's the seriously strong cocktails as foam rises in my mouth. I have no option to spew it into the sea as Spiro scoops a handful of salt water and smears it over my mouth. It hasn't fazed him one bit as he takes my arm and drags me out, pushing forward against the waves.

'Ela, come Ruby. We walk further along to Kalamaki,' he instructs as he retrieves our clothes from the sand. And then he says something in such a matter-of-fact manner that it instantly sobers me up. 'Ela, Kalamaki will be quieter and will be a good place to make sex.'

'

The sea and beach are at peace with itself again as Aphrodite retreats and we stroll, linking arms. The hazy moonlight guides us along and my ears ask themselves did they hear Spiro's last comment correctly.

Twenty or so blissful minutes later, we arrive where the beach merges into Kalamaki.
'Here, now. I understand that this is the spot where you rested and waited till sunrise,' he reminds me as I spot the tired sunbeds on their side.
'But we will disturb the hatchlings at this time of night,' I say as he turns a sunbed flat and guides me down onto it with his strong hands.
'No Ruby. The hatchlings will not be disturbed by us. It is only when there are a lot of feet stamping on the sand that they feel the vibrations. It is not like they

all come out together. Each chelona, turtle make their own journey alone as it is necessary for them to use the moon to set their own magnetic compass, so we will not see a big family of turtles all at once. Another piece of information you may find interesting is the sex of the chelona depends on the temperature of the sand. If I remember right, I think it is the ladies that like it hot! If the temperature is 29 degrees plus, the sex will be female, if lower, it will be male.'

'Oh, that's really interesting as I like it hot too,' I cringe inwardly at the cliché, but it works as he lays me down on the sunbed and he lifts my face to his. The stars are out in earnest as we gaze up at them from our vantage point and he points out the constellations. All I want is him, as I guide his body on mine. The glass in my heart, the result of my guilt of endangering the turtles, is replaced by satin as I take him inside me.

He's softly snoring against my chest as I lie there sated and relieved. A dark object brushes by in the sand, but this time I have no fear.

4   Island adventure

Zante Town – heading for the hills
Adeline and Ruby
It's midday as the two girls hop off the bus from Laganas, in front of the impressive church of Agios Dionysios in Zante town.

Adeline, as fresh as a daisy from an uninterrupted sleep, but still hurting from the departure of Walter, takes the lead as they march down the main promenade next to the port, which reaches out to curve round to almost touch the lighthouse on the other side.

Ruby struggles to keep pace as an overwhelming weariness takes over her body as her head spins like a wheel full of images of last night's shenanigans and the disparaging eyes that would have seen them sloping back to the hotel, on their return to the hotel.

In the second it takes for her to slump on the conveniently located bench, her thoughts are with Spiro; she longs to be in his arms again, making love under the shimmering moon and flickering stars.

Adeline marches on like an army major; oblivious that Ruby is laid out on the bench still thinking of the night before when they had returned to the Angel Hotel.

The long stroll back from Kalamaki had sobered her up but given her options to muse over. Glad that she worked a bar while travelling, she was intent on making an impression as she coaxed Spiro to open his bar as she deftly proved her cocktail making skills, in the hope he would consider her for the bar vacancy. But when he ran his lips over his mouth in approval, sensibility took over her salacious thoughts. It's so tempting to stay on the idyllic island with Spiro, but she needs to prioritise her life and make some profound changes.

As the sea breeze caresses her face, she knows she must take a leaf out of her cousin's book and be a responsible adult after two whirlwind whimsical years of travelling. She feels like a drop of water in the ocean of life, a mere speck of matter. The angel of reason tells her she needs to grow up, focus on a career, invest in property, and climb the corporate ladder. Regrettably, the devil of desire did not make an appearance!

'Ruby! I thought you were right behind me,' Adeline yells as she turns round and approaches the bench, with far too much energy for Ruby's liking. 'Come on piss pot, let's get something to eat and then you can reveal all!'

They cross the main road to a lone taverna, with green and white gingham tablecloths.

'It's so beautiful here. Could you imagine living here in a capital city and it being as pleasant as this? Ruby comments as she pulls the spoon out of the Greek yoghurt and honey.

'I know. It is seriously gorgeous. Nearly as gorgeous as Walter! I wonder where he is now?' Ruby takes her cousin's hand and squeezes it in understanding, her thoughts also on Spiro and what could have been.

They tuck into the cheese and spinach pies. Flakes fall to the ground as the resident cats lap them up. After a few minutes of quiet contemplation, Ruby takes a sweep of their surroundings.

'Look around us Addie. Isn't it just gorgeous?'

'It is Ruby, it is,' she replies, lowering her sunglasses and following the curvature of the promenade.

'Look over there to the port and how the hills curve round with it. And can you see those small hillocks rolling gracefully down the hills, looking like they are forming a queue.

'Oh Ruby, imagine living here, breathing in all this pure air.'

As Ruby nods her agreement, she continues her geographical observations noting how at the end of the town an exposed rock escarpment lies on its side, blanketed in green, abruptly stopping where the Venetian buildings grace the promenade.

''Ruby, would you like to stay here on the island for a while longer or are you hanging up your travel boots?' Ruby doesn't respond as she excuses herself in search of the toilet.

'Mmm, well now I have got rid of all that alcohol, I'm all yours again Addie! And in answer to your question – Yes it must be lovely to live here. What a different take on life we would have, rather than battling with the motorway traffic around Manchester every weekday.'

Lost in their own thoughts, they both notice a group of sun-kissed children as they ride their bikes along the promenade with brightly coloured kites trailing behind them. How carefree their childhoods must be, they muse.

'Koritsia. Girls. Are you looking for a hotel? I see you have your small luggage with you,' asks the stocky waiter as he returns with the bill and some pastries, wrapped loosely in a napkin.

'Yes. We are, but not too expensive,' Ruby answers as Adeline refocuses her attention.

'Ok I will make a map for you. One moment please.' He reaches over to the adjacent table and starts to draw lines on a scrap of paper. 'You walk a short way to the left until you get to the main Solomos Square. It is a gathering spot with a few monuments. Follow the road that leads to the interior. This is Kourtsoula. Then take a left to Apolophanis then to Pikridiotissis. You will come to a small church – the church of Saint Dimitrios of Kanesi. This is where I was baptised. Opposite this church you will see a small hotel, the Hotel Eleni. This belongs to my mother-in-law, Kiria

Eleni. I will phone her now to say you will be there soon and she will give you a nice room with a view to the castle on the hill or it may be a side view of the sea.'

What should take twenty minutes, following the makeshift map takes them an hour as the sun hovers high in the sky and penetrates the earth like a laser. Ruby is desperate to rest her sleep deprived body, struggling to cope in the searing heat.

For want of a rest she stops to read an information plaque.

'So, this is Paul Karrer a noble prize Russian chemist. In 1931, he succeeded in extracting vitamin A from Cod Liver oil. In 1933, he determined the structure of vitamin B2 which made it possible to produce the vitamin by artificial means.'

'Very interesting but I think we may need to get a move on, or Eleni may think we've changed our minds and give the room away.

Eventually, after a few wrong turns and rest breaks they stumble upon the church as a young teenage boy whistles them over to the Hotel Eleni. A sprightly middle- aged lady with a white streak in her hair waves from a balcony, beckoning them to come in, 'Ela, ela - come, come.'

'The teenager resumes his duty of checking them in with his perfect English, handing them a bottle of water each.

'You have the choice of a room with a side view of the sea or the view of the ruins of the Bochali Venetian Castle. I would recommend the castle view,' he recommends as he hovers over the wooden board where the keys hang, pre-empting which room they will choose.

'Oh, this is much better Ruby. Better than that awful basement. I think you could use a nap cousin before we go and hire a moped.'

Ruby is face flat on the single bed, snoring her hangover away. Adeline makes herself comfortable on the wrought iron balcony, soaking up the view to the castle and the abundant olive groves that blanket the incline in an emerald green.

Two hours later
With a renewed sense of vigour, they make their way back into town each with a small backpack, stuffed with the necessities for a ride around the island. And although both girls are secretly thinking about a certain male each, they try to shrug it off as best they can and enjoy their island adventure.

'Do you both like to ride?' the white-haired man in the office asks as he urges them to katsi, katsi -sit, sit and a younger male, most likely his grandson, sets down three Greek coffees cups, accompanied by a small serving of lemon cake and a tiny silver spoon. 'Yiayia made the cake this morning,' he informs them, smiling from ear to ear as his long dark fringe flops over his eyes.

'It's just me riding. Here's my licence,' Ruby says as she selects a Honda 50 from the glossy pictures sellotaped to the desk.

'No problem, Miss Ruby Royle. This is good name, I think. I like it. My name is much longer. I am Theodore Papachristodoulopoulos. It means someone who is a servant of the Lord Christ and descendant of the Priest,' he explains tilting his head back slightly and raising his eyes to the ceiling as if conferring with the Lord Christ himself.

Both girls animate their astonishment as the grandson leads them to their shiny red mode of transport for the next three days.

'Please a map of our island and I make circle of places of interest and the stations for the petrol. Please be careful and wear your hats,' he says in a well-rehearsed and articulated spiel.

'Please could you show me the controls and where the petrol goes,' asks Ruby, just before he returns inside the air-conditioned office. Eager to practise his English he gives them a full demonstration, pointing to the various parts of the moped and asking for an English translation.

From the other side of the road at the side of the promenade a lone taxi and a lone man are watching the girls every move.

Demetrius Pappas

I spend my life behind this goddam wheel. I should have been spending my working hours behind a highly polished walnut desk. By now, I would have had my own chartered accountants with professionals under my supervision - raking in the drachmas with a sumptuous villa hugging the cliffs and overlooking the azure Ionian seas. Thanks, or rather no thanks, to that malaka Manolis, my office is my tired taxi, and my home is a wooden shack I share with my goats up in the hills and as a result of my injuries, I will never be able to learn anything new. Each day and night is a living hell as I will my stupid brain to remember the roads of my island. The roads

I knew like the back of my hand in my youth - the roads that I rode my beloved motorbike on with my many girlfriends as they wrapped their arms around in panda bear embraces, finding the hollow in my back with their ample chests -until I could take no more and drive my bike into the nearest olive grove while I had my way with them.

Regrettably, in my youthful ignorance, I admit I went too far with a few. My alter ego kicked in and I may have been a little rough and then when the act was finished, I would look down at them sobbing on the ground - my body had been possessed by the devil. I left them there bleeding and bruised, knowing that they would have a long stumble to the nearest village to ask for help, knowing that the following day there would be a manhunt after me. Inevitably, on a small island I would be found immediately. That's when they sent me to Athens – to the psychiatric unit. Dark days followed while they tried to figure me out and make me whole again. They did eventually and I was allowed back on my island.

Two hours after arriving, my family sent me into hiding, up in the hills. A few weeks went by as I began to feel at ease again and I made the basic wooden shack my home, with only goats for company. That is when the attack happened. They had hunted me down. He had beaten me to a pulp. My life would never be the same again.

Walter

I couldn't do it. I couldn't leave all this beauty and freedom behind. I know there are other islands to explore, other cultures to experience and other people to meet. But the moment I stepped foot in the airport, I knew it was too soon to leave. There's just something about Zante. It's intoxicating. From the hedonism to the tranquillity, I need to explore every little piece of the rugged coastline of the southwest and the mountainous plateau of the west. To venture into the interior and meet the villagers who don't speak English. It would be good to be taken out of my comfort zone and to be forced to use the Greek phrases Maria taught me at the Minimart, just to be understood. Hell, I've not even taken a boat to the famous shipwreck on Navagio beach or swam around the myriads of natural blue caves or even tried to swim to Marathonisi Island where the famous turtles breed just off Laganas.

And now the lovely Adeline, as if by fate, is almost looking in my direction, hopping on a moped that her cousin is struggling to start up. I resist the temptation to race over and help as that would seem too eager. I watch as they set off and nearly collide with an ice cream cart, making its way around the corner.

Demetrius Pappas

Only a few yards away from Walter, Demetrius Pappas ruminates on his next move. He is still fuming with these stupid English tourist girls. In fact, he hates all the tourist girls who visit his island -

showing too much flesh down on the beach and even here in Zante Town. Then they complain when they get the whistles from the hot bloodied males. He hates it when they get in his taxi and demand he speaks in English and talks to him like some kaka on their shoes. He wants to physically hit them when they complain that he is taking the long way round to their destination, as if they know his island better than him.

Then just three nights ago, in the early hours of the morning, these two bitches got into his taxi at the airport and demanded he take them to the beach. To add to his frustration, he found it hard to remember his way from the airport to Kalamaki, where he knew the hotel would give him some commission. It was a relief that they were none the wiser as to the distance to the resort and a relief that he had eventually found his way there, even though it was a mere three kilometres away. His odometer, which he zeroed for each trip, read ten kilometres!

Furthermore, Demetrius was fuming when he could not think of the English word for chelona when the cocky girl demanded he dropped them at the beach. For once in his life, he wasn't just thinking of himself – he was also worried they would disturb the nesting turtles on the beach. It was a miracle story how the chelona spawn in the same beach it was born. Demetrius knew how important it was to keep people off the beaches at night from June to August, when the females reach the beach to spawn.

His blood boiled further when the stupid tourist girls, who thought he owed them something, were endangering his island with their superior attitude. *Did they not read and learn about his island before they arrived? Did they not know that the younglings made their tentative journey to the sea following the horizon and moonlight that reflected off the water? Did they not know that by shining a torch they would disorientate the younglings and with only a small percentage of hatchlings actually surviving that first journey, they were contributing to their extinction?*

Then there was the humiliation when one of the bitches stamped on his toes and the other silly bitch thought she could speak Greek as she threw his fare at him.

Beads of sweat formed on his forehead. His hands gripped his steering wheel and spurred on by some out of body force, he pulled out of the parking bay and took the inland road, keeping the red moped in his vision. He hadn't noticed Walter. And likewise, Walter hadn't noticed Demetrius.

Three days previously - Zante Police station

Two hours after Demetrius had dropped the girls at Kalamaki beach, he drove straight to the police station in Zante Town. It took him so long as he took the wrong road in the completely wrong direction. Fortunately for him, his island was relatively small and no matter how many times he lost his way, he would always return to base – eventually.

'Pah! That malaka Demetrius Pappas has made a complaint again,' huffed the police officer manning the front desk, as he sipped his second frappe of the morning. He had a long shift ahead of him and as his insomnia had returned with a vengeance, he knew the caffeine would help him through his shift.

'Now what does he complain about? Does he not remember he has amnesia?' replied his colleague, as he lit up his third cigarette of the morning. 'What does he report this time? His goat that someone has poisoned? The feta cheese he thinks has been stolen from his dirty little wooden shack?'

'Today is more serious. He reports there are two girl tourists who are endangering our chelona,'

'This is more serious then.'

'Yes, it is but you know how he is with his memory. He reported that he picked them up at four in the morning at the airport and they had nowhere to stay so he took them to Kalamaki. They would not take the offer of the hotel room and screamed at him to drop them at the beach. They used force on him, kicked at him then ran down to the beach without paying the fare.'

'Maybe they are the same two girls? Maybe they are up to no good after all? His colleague swept away a small red beetle on his files as he took a long drag of his cigarette.

'Yes, maybe they are. Tell Adonis to follow them even more closely. It is probably nothing, but we must do our job to protect the island and the chelona.'

The Renta Moped office – Zante Town

'So, you are familiar with riding a moped?' Theodore Papachristopoulos asks Walter as he hands him the keys. He notices the young blond man's hands shake a little as he takes the keys from him.

'Yes, I am, thank you. I am riding around the island as it is my last day on holiday. Tell me please where the more independent tourists would ride to when they are exploring the island?' Walter's throat is parched as he struggles to say the last few words. He knows he is coming across a little suspicious and nervous, but he needs to know which part of the island the girls may have said they were heading.

'Ahh, so you have some interest in the koritisia that hire the red moped?'

'How do you know that?' Walter asks, taken off guard, retrieving some coins in his pocket for the vending machine. The orangeade drops with a thud from the metal claws. He scoops it from the tray and hastily drinks it. He's never known such thirst as he has, while on the island.

'I see you opposite next to the taxi. I see you watching the girls. Tell me, do you have feelings for one of them? Do you know them? I do not know in which direction they go. I hope you find them. Ride careful and don't forget to wear your hat. The roads here they get extremely hot and slippery.'

Just as Walter rides away, the young boy offers him a map, adding,

'The girls on the red moped. They ask me how far to the Venetian wells.'

Studying the map, out of sight of the office, Walter traces his finger from Zante Town to the site of the ancient Venetian wells. He calculates they are about twenty kilometres away, near enough straight across to the southwest of the island. The inland road will take him over and past the bay of Laganas and over to the cliffs of Plakaki beach, passing through the rustic villages of Lithakia and Agalas. Set back from the cliffs, surrounded by vineyards, he makes a circle with a pen around the remote wells which, are also known as the Andronios wells.

The stone in the pit of his stomach relays that he needs to find them very soon; he fears for the girls' safety. He hopes that Ruby is a proficient moped rider, and that Adeline will hold on securely to her cousin. Walter has always gone off his gut feeling. So far it has never let him down.

Manolis and Spiros - Laganas

My head is full of barbed wire. It feels heavy and burdened. I need to speak to my cousin Spiros on my way back to Zante Town. The trouble is, I have been so busy with the vermin, trying to keep them under control before the tourists find out and flee the island. Then where would we be? The famous Zante currants we export, along with the olives, are not enough to keep us going all year round. If the word gets out and spreads to the travel industry, we are doomed. Maybe I feel like there's another force weighing me down because of my workload. Spiros will make sense of it all.

I pull into the hotel driveway. It's siesta time, so the main road down to the beach is sleepy except for a few groups of young men drinking beer from cans, wearing identical bright T- shirts, that have big letters across their chests – I'm not very good with the English alphabet but I think the names say Dicky, Cocky, Nobby and some more I can't quite read. I find my cousin behind his desk in the cool marble reception.

'Kalispera Spiro. I have something on my chest apart from my hairs,' I say, knowing my cousin will break into a smile and direct us to the bar area. The swimming pool is flat and empty, except for a few bright pink phallic looking inflatables the guests have abandoned in their haste to retreat from the oppressive heat. A few groups of guests are languishing in the covered bar area as I spot a bartender with neat blond hair, vigorously cutting up some pineapple. He is a good-looking man, I think to myself.

'Manolis. What is it you have on your hairy chest?' my cousin asks as he instructs his bartender to whip up two frappes – without the pummelled pineapple! He nods his head and smiles as he searches for the correct glasses to use. I can imagine it must be overwhelming to be thrown behind a bar and work your way around the drinks and other stuff. Much to the bemusement of many people, when I tell them my profession, I would rather work on my own and have the satisfaction that, no matter how gruesome it can be, catching vermin also has a cathartic effect.

'Spiro,' I answer, as he prompts me to speak. 'Ahh, yes. My reason for coming at this hour is I need to get a niggle off my hairy chest again. Spiro. I have this feeling in my bones that the girls are still in danger. It's like a dull ache in my bones all day, every day since they arrived, and I picked them up on the road from Kalamaki.'

'Manolis they have left very eagerly this morning,' my cousin informs me with a glisten in his eyes. My heart is racing as I push my frappe to one side. The doctor told me not to overdo the caffeine with my condition. He also told me not to worry about every little thing, but it's not as easy as that. Since I found out about the attack on my wife and as long as the malaka is on the island, I will never stop worrying.

'But Spiro why did you let them leave? I need to find them.' I know it's not my cousin's fault, after all, he is not their Greek guardian, and so I apologise and thank him for the frappe. He scratches his head and shrugs his shoulders as I start my pickup. He bobs his head through the open window.

'Manolis. the other night I take the dark-haired girl Ruby back to Kalamaki beach to try to ease her conscience. She feels much better now. I honestly do not think they are in danger. Ruby tells me she has travelled all over the world and has been in some sticky situations before, even here in Greece. She says she is like a cat with nine lives. Please do not worry. Remember your Yiatro says you must not get anxious. Love your heart,' my cousin pleads as I start my truck, bid him farewell and return to Zante Town.

Fortunately, I have many contacts here in the capital. I start with the hotels, guessing they will go for the cheaper ones set back from the main road and promenade. It takes me only half an hour to locate the affordable Hotel Eleni that my wife's friend owns. Eleni confirms the girls are staying there for a few nights.

'Can you keep your eye on the girls. Give me a ring as soon as they return. I should be in my workshop most of the day.' Eleni is an astute woman with a good sense of character.

'Of course, Manolis. They are nice enough girls. They left about an hour ago. Then they returned to pick up something from their room on a red moped. Here write down your work telephone number, I only have your home number. How is my dear friend Ariadne?'

'She is well, thanking you Eleni.' Just as I'm about to drive off to scour the multitude of moped hire offices near the harbour walls, Eleni waves for me to stop again.

'Manolis are your concerns connected to Demetrius Pappas?' I nod my head as I force a reassuring smile and navigate the short route, through the narrow alleys onto the main promenade road.

It takes me ten minutes to find the office and thankfully it is my good friend Theodore who confirms they have rented the red moped from him.

'But I do not know where they are heading Manolis. Tourists usually stick to the coast road, but my grandson Thassos gave them a map. He may know. Oh hell, he has gone for his afternoon walk now. It was too quiet, so I sent him for some air.'

Adrenaline courses through my body as I wrack my brains to decipher where they may have headed. Even though it is a small island, there are still many remote and secluded areas where even the most adventurous tourists never stumble upon, let alone locals. Amazingly I catch sight of Thassos, marching down the promenade as I screech to a halt.

'Thassos. Remember me? I am your grandfather's friend Manolis. I need your help.

'Yes, Manolis I did speak to them. They are heading to the Venetian wells. They said they wanted to see the interior of the island. I hope I have said the right thing, Manolis. There was another man asking me the same – if I knew where the girls are heading. Are they in trouble?'

'This other man. What did he look like Thassos?'

'He had a big black baseball cap on covering most of his face. He isn't Greek though, but I noticed he had one of those girly bags strapped round his waist. He also hired a moped this morning,' Thassos explains as he rubs his hands together – a habit from his schooldays when he was forever in trouble for his slight stammer.

'Don't worry Thassos and thank you,' I reassure him, as I get my bearings and drive towards the national road across to the southwest coast. Timing is all I have as I break the island speed limit and hope I get there in time. Who the hell is the other moped driver with the baseball cap and girl bag?

Walter

I know that I shouldn't be following them, but I know that the young boy in the moped hire office would not be able to divulge where they are staying. So, this is my only option. I need to know they are safe. I have a troubling feeling in my blood. I need to explain to Adeline why I didn't say goodbye to her.

I lose my concentration for a moment and remember the few snatched moments holding her tight. In the six months I have been on the island, I have kept my pact with myself. Still, I have not allowed myself to become involved with both males and females. Yet my heart still yearns for Adeline. And now it is almost too good to be true – she is here still and so close but so far away.

With the image of the lovely Adeline swimming around in my head, I lose my focus again. Disorientated and unable to spot any signposts for the wells, I steer the rigid moped around a hairpin bend until the road is straight again, but I can't decide whether to turn right or left or carry straight on. I look at the map while one hand steers. I feel I have gone too far as the shrubbery gets thicker and I find myself riding deeper into the olive groves. They won't have taken this dirt path, so I turn around and continue straight. If only there was a signpost, and I could see the red moped.

The back story   1969-1972

Zante Town Hospital   January 1972

Name of victim: Demetrius Pappas

Age of victim: 21

Name of perpetrator: unknown

Location of attack: Black Cave Kallithea 290 90

Zakynthos Greece

Approximate time of attack: 4 am

Injuries sustained: Blow to the front and back of skull.

Unfortunately, for Demetrius Pappas, the attack at the Black Cave, located in the interior of the island, 100 metres above the fertile plain resulted in amnesia. Further tests were performed to determine the extent of the injury, whereby they concluded that the victim could be suffering from both anterograde and retrograde amnesia. Anterograde amnesia presents the inability to create new memories and a difficulty holding on to new information. Retrograde amnesia presents as the inability to recall events that happened just before the event that led to amnesia. Thus, the familiar male who carried out the attack on Demetrius Pappas could never be recalled as a memory. If the victim had of been of good character and not had a chequered history, the police in Zante Town may have searched more thoroughly for his attacker. Instead, Demetrius Pappas' statement made its way to file 13 - the paper basket.

Months of bedrest and a definite confirmation of amnesia forced Demetrius to abandon his studies to qualify as an accountant. A year later, a generous anonymous payment was made to the family to purchase a car to start his own taxi business. What his distraught and heartbroken parents didn't envisage was the prolonged effect of their only son's amnesia, as he had to learn from scratch, the roads of his island.

Spring 1969

Ariadne Papadimitriou

Although I have been warned about Demetrius Pappas, I just can't get him out of my head. He's not asked me for a date yet, but I know the way he looks my way in church, it won't be long. Like him, church bores me as my eyes and thoughts wander around the congregation, wondering why I don't feel the spiritualism of Papas Tsitak as he wails and chants, throwing holy water all over our Sunday best. People are most peculiar I reason, as I watch the local doctor as his puppy eyes beg to be acknowledged in the eyes of the papas. The reverence between both doctor and priest is surely reciprocating? I stifle a yawn just as Demetrius catches my eye again, and the blood rushes to my cheeks. I fear the papas can read my mind, as thoughts of Demetrius will not go away.

The next Sunday, Demetrius is behind me. His eyes bore into my back. *How does one male, who I cannot even see as I stand at the front of him, make me feel like this?* Mitera mou turns my way as I wanly smile at her, hoping she hasn't caught me dreaming and not paying attention to the papas. My mother is the matriarch; hence nothing gets past her. She knows instinctively the subtlest of signs that may be a cause for concern with each of her five children. If Demetrius does ask me for a date, I will have to have a cunning plan but I'm sure it will be worth it.

Demetrius Pappas

The sensation of silk sends me in frenzy. Ariadne, no doubt has borrowed her older sister's underdress as I remember the amber colour and the dainty lace around the hem. If her sister hadn't resisted my touch that evening, she might have been still dating me. She is far too frigid for my liking and a little on the plain side. Although she did have a voluptuous body, it was important I had to break up with her before she complained about my sexual advances.

Then a few months later, that's when I spotted her younger sister in church. I feel that I can easily manipulate her and hopefully she will comply more than her sister did. I assume her sister had been too humiliated when I dumped her to reveal she had ever dated me. Thus, I felt I was safe with Ariadne. Unlike the others, she will not run.

The day is bright as are most days on my island. However, today, nothing is clouding my vision. I feel the pureness of the air more, the sparkling sea that is visible from almost any of the vantage points of the island and the soothing May sunshine that will make this a day I will never forget. Today I will get my girl.

My uncle's wooden shack is not the most comfortable and pretty of places to take a girl, but it is the perfect place to take Ariadne after we have climbed up to the Black Cave. And although it may be cold and damp, even in April, the view from this vantage point is breath taking. From the 200-metre height, the lush green groves of olives and grapevines, interspersed with slim Cypress trees, directs the eye towards the cobalt waters of the Ionian Sea. Like many other islanders, there is a high probability that Ariadne has never been here before.

How lucky I am to be born on the island, I remind myself. On the downside, it is a smallish island and gossip spreads like an unwelcome storm, resulting in every Tomas, Ricardos and Haris knowing your God damned business. And in my case, regrettably, my kamaki history is not of the favourable kind. But if Ariadne conforms to my advances, I may be able to ditch my bad kamaki image and resurrect a new me –

Demetrius Pappas, the best lover a girl could ever wish for. We would eventually marry after I have returned from university and secured a good career in accountancy and bought a comfortable property, ideally overlooking the cliffs. I want to be no younger than thirty before I have children of my own. Only then will I consider bringing my offspring into the world.

Yesterday I came up to my uncle's shack which is where he spends most of his shepherding and goat herding days and nights. Yesterday he left the island for a few days to attend a funeral over in Patras on the mainland, so I've brought my bedding and a few cushions to scatter around. There is only myself and my uncle who use the shack and we are the only ones that know its whereabouts. The interior is basic - just a wobbly table, accompanied by two wobbly, wooden chairs, a ceramic bowl for washing in, a straw bed and earth on the floor is all that adorns it.

So, I'll light a few citronellas to mask the smell of the goats and hopefully, just as it begins to turn dusk and we have hiked across from the Black Cave, the sunset will cast subtle hues of orange and reds and soften the harshness and emptiness of the interior. Then I will pour us both a glass of the finest wine made from the grapes that grow in the fertile soils of my family's grapevines. When the grapes are full and bursting off their vines, my family and I pick them before my papa takes them to the village winery to be pressed into the sweetest wine. I will serve this to Ariadne, and it will be like honey to a bee – smooth and sweet. Hopefully, she will get a taste for my nectar and after a few more glasses, she will give herself to me. She will be mine. It may be nice if she makes the first move though, as I reciprocate her kisses and she pulls me to the bed, unable to suppress her lust for me.

Instinctively, I raise my head to the Lord himself and ask for forgiveness from the other girls I have mistreated and promise Ariadne will be the one I care for all of my life.

7pm that evening

My plan worked. We lie side by side on the thin mattress on top of the straw bales, wrapped in each other's arms in a bid to be close to each other but to also stop us from falling on the earth below. I was amazed that Ariadne actually embraced the transformed wooden shack and as I had envisaged, the setting sun has worked its magic. Ariadne is meant to be mine. From the moment I saw her, even as a younger girl stood next to her sister in church, I knew she was the one; the special woman that would actually make me realise I am a good person.

Tonight, I am a very grateful and a happy man. And it is with great reluctance that I blow out the candles and drive her back home. This day has been the best day of my life. Glass runs through my blood and pierces my lungs as I struggle to breathe. The reason

I feel this way is because soon I will have to leave the island to travel to Patras, to pursue my studies.

Ariadne - Early Summer of '69

Our passionate first date up at the wooden shack left me delirious. He and my sister are not aware that I know they also dated before me. Did he take her to the wooden shack and lay her down on that surprisingly comfortable straw bed? My thoughts should repulse me, but I feel the opposite. I feel that the reason he cast my sister aside was because he wanted her younger sister. My sister Maria has not inherited our mother's striking looks. Luckily, I have. The boys in the village whisper how they cannot believe I am from the same genes. '*How is her younger sister so beautiful like a blossoming mountain flower – wild and free spirited with sensual eyes,*' they ask each other in the village square where they group together on balmy evenings, kicking up stones with their bicycles, wishing they were kamakis on mopeds.

Unfortunately, my sister emulates a downtrodden woman, old and plain before her years, dressed in dowdy colours with a broom permanently stuck to her hands.

Maybe one day I can teach her how to attract the men. That is of course when I turn eighteen next spring, and we can reveal our courtship. But for now, we will continue in secrecy and make the most of our snatched afternoons and early evenings up at the wooden shack, whenever Demetrius's uncle is away.

Although many of my friends are married and are now bearing children, my parents veer away from tradition. Mitera and Patera mou both have successful careers and are disappointed that my older sister did not want to further her education so they have high hopes for me. They have secured a scholarship for me to attend Law next spring in

Patras. How can I tell them I don't want to leave the island and my secret love? How can I disclose that, although I am academic and studying comes easy to me, I actually have no desire to become a slave to my career with sleepless nights and stressful days? My island is part of my whole existence. Material things do not matter to me. Even the wooden shack which holds so many wonderful memories in the arms of Demetrius, would be enough for me. And I think Demetrius is of the same opinion - he has not mentioned about furthering his career or moving from the island like so many younger people in search of free love and drugs do. So, when I reveal next month, when I have missed two periods and I am with child, I hope that he will sweep me in his strong arms and shower me with kisses – kisses so hard that my face will eventually sting as he lays me on the bed and feels my swelling stomach and the little life inside me. The life we have made together.

Before Demetrius met Ariadne.

It is as if a demon possesses my mind and body. I beat them for no reason. I am demonised as in my rage this alter ego takes control as my fists lay into their soft bodies. It is only when the crimson blood spills onto the earth, do I stop. Depending on my situation and where we are on the island, I either run for it and leave them writhing and clutching their broken bodies or I take them in my arms and carefully bathe their wounds, telling them everything will be fine as long as they don't tell a soul.

The others I run from must be so humiliated that they too don't tell a soul. It takes a few days for my alter ego to depart my mind. In those demonised days I hide in the hills, frightened of what I may do, frightened that I may be found out.

Late Summer 1969

Ariadne was my first true love. After all, she has made me a man. It is such a shame that she has tricked me. I always made a point in asking if it was the right time on the calendar. We hadn't broached the subject of the possibility of her becoming pregnant. Unfortunately, my alter ego presented itself again as her face and stomach felt the heavy blow of my fist. We were in the wooden shack that afternoon as the low autumnal sun found a crack in the thin curtains and warmed our naked bodies as she took my hand and placed it on her slightly rounded stomach. And then she whispered the words that my alter ego never wanted to hear.

Like her sister before her, humiliation must have taken over the urge to report me. It still frightens me. I frighten myself. I am frightened at the prospect that I will, one day be found out -that they will all come together and testify that I, Demetrius Pappas, is a coward and a woman beater. But now I am fathering her unborn baby. Maybe I should end it all now or leave for Patras?

Two years later 1971

Manolis and Ariadne

Since the attack, Ariadne has not felt comfortable around males. She yearns to offload her guilt with someone but knows it will be futile. Unfortunately, she blames herself for her attack. It transpires she read the signs wrong. Why did Demetrius never mention he didn't want children? Why did she assume that although they were careful to avoid pregnancy, his initial shock would soon subside and he would be overjoyed with the news? After all, they were truly and deeply in love.

Thus, it takes her almost two years to even look at another male, apart from the males in her family.

Her parents are devastated. They had high hopes for their younger daughter – university leading to a professional career. As they don't know the real reason for Ariadne's voluntary solitary confinement, they are unable to figure out a solution. They pray each day and seek solace in Papas Tsitak that through their prayers, their little girl will shine once more, graduate from university and make them proud.

It was only when Marina, Ariadne's best friend who is now married to the village baker with two children to care for, took time out from her hectic domestic schedule and visited Ariadne in her bedroom that had become her prison.

The next week Marina asked her mother to look after little Anastasia and Penelope. She knew it was sneaky but she knew that her cousin Manolis was single and the gentlest man anyone could ever meet. So, one chilly spring day, Marina picked up her friend from her village in the hills and reintroduced her to the sights and sounds of their picturesque capital city.

Manolis had been given the whereabouts of a few coffee shops they may choose from and was told to observe from a distance until he received the subtle sign from Marina. Fortunately, for Manolis, he liked what he saw as he peeked over the menu from where he sat at on the other side of the café. He had forgotten his glasses and had to get much closer than he should have, much to the slight annoyance of Marina. He listened to the song on the jukebox, Hotel California by the Eagles and realised that he'd never been in a bar quite like this. He'd always hung out in the kafenions, playing backgammon and discussing politics with the older men. As he looked around the trendy café at the young women with long flowing skirts and psychedelic tie- dyed tops, he understood why he was still single.

But it was Ariadne who caught his eye. Dressed in a simple flowery dress with a pink shawl wrapped round her slim shoulders as if to protect her vulnerability, she was the most natural young woman he'd ever had the pleasure to set eyes upon.

It was a match. Marina congratulated herself at setting up the perfect blind date. And although she never revealed it to her friend, they both knew each other too well for Ariadne to think that it had all happened by happenstance.

After a few more dates, on their own of course, Manolis and Ariadne had definitely been struck by the thunderbolt and were now truly a couple. As both sets of parents were from good stock, owning many businesses between them, the eventual resurrection from her recluse, was well received by both families.

The truth revealed:

The time eventually arrives when Ariadne is able to offload her guilty secret. Manolis is a raging bull the

moment she reveals her attacker's name.
Regrettably, the consequences are disastrous. In a matter of a couple of days of careful planning with an alibi set up, Manolis leaves his pickup along the olive groves, set back from the main road. He then covers his head and most of his face with a baseball cap and wraps a dark green, full-length jacket around him. He chooses some old shoes which are so worn they have no tread. However, he is a nimble man and knows he can steady himself on the steep climb up to the Black Cave. When he reaches the top, he takes a sharp right along a narrow weed infested track which leads down to the wooden shack. If there is no sign of him there, there have been many sightings of him down in Zante Town, where he is said to loiter around the tourist bars that have sprung up in the back streets.

That morning, Ariadne warns Manolis that a verbal attack would be far more constructive than a physical attack. However, she senses her plea has fallen on deaf ears.

It seems too good to be true as Manolis approaches the wooden shack and spots Demetrius with his back to him, working on some rope on a plastic stool outside. By nature, he isn't a violent man, and he hasn't laid a finger on anyone in his life before. But the mere sight of the man who had beaten up his girlfriend and killed her baby, is too much to bear as he takes him by surprise and lays into him like an antagonised bear with his bare fists.

The next day, by a stroke of luck for his survival, Demetrius's uncle returns early from the other side of the island. Upon finding his nephew battered and bloodied, slumped to the ground, with hardly a pulse, he races back down to the nearest village and calls the hospital. As the location of the shack is inaccessible by vehicle, he summons the help of the fitter males as they swiftly make a wooden stretcher, retreat up to the shack and bring the barely alive battered body of his nephew back down to the village, to await an ambulance.

Demetrius spends many months in the hospital and fortunately for Manolis, Ariadne and the reputation of their families, the amnesia he sustained means that he will probably never be able to recall the identity of his attacker.

A few months later, Ariadne and Manolis make an appointment with the Yiatro. The family doctor is quite perplexed at their request. He has never had such a request before. The young couple ask for some tests that may confirm if Ariadne is able to bear children. Yiatros Diplomatasi is aghast at the results from the hospital, confirming that there is damage to Ariadne's reproductive organs that may suggest the chances of an embryo surviving is highly unlikely. *How has Ariadne sustained these injuries, he wants to know*? Somehow, he doesn't believe her when she says she had had a nasty fall down her stairs three years previously.

Despite the disappointing news, Manolis and Ariadne are married a few months later. Contrary to what most folk assume the reason for their hasty marriage, is their deep love for each other and not because she is with child. Unfortunately, that is no longer a possibility.

There is no doubt though that it will be on the minds and tongues of many people who know them both: *'Are you with child yet? When shall we start knitting for baby? Are you hoping for many babies?* etc. etc.

Manolis and Ariadne know beforehand that they will have to endure the relentless enquiries and after a year or so into their marriage with no signs of a pregnancy, word will spread between villagers that it must either be her or him who cannot reproduce. Thus, upon having two homes to choose from, a wedding present from Ariadne's parents, they choose to move away from their village at the foot of the Vrachionas mountain and move 10 kilometres south to near Zante Town. The cottage itself is situated on a slight slope, looking down to the Ionian Sea where the Argassi Bridge, half submerged in water, resembles a prehistoric water monster, rising up from the depths. They settle well in their new home, only returning to their village for family occasions.

---

5   Present day - Chase to the Venetian Wells

Walter

By a stroke of luck, I catch up with the red moped lying on its side in a clearing in the middle of the lush olive groves. Rows of ground level circular holes tell me I must be at the Venetian wells. *But where are they and why have they just dumped the moped? Surely, they know they are responsible for the hire and for any damage?* I spot a taxi parked opposite, under the shade of the olive trees. Deducing that some other tourists are also sightseeing and have paid for a taxi ride, I park up, take my helmet off and begin to search around the wells. If the girls see me, I can pretend I am here by chance, doing a little sightseeing myself.

Just as I'm glancing down one of the wells to see if they are still in operation, I hear a scream from the other side of the clearing which is unmistakably a woman's if not Adeline's. My heart jumps to my throat as I stop myself from shouting out. I fear there is someone behind me. Instinctively, I crouch down and cover my head with my hands. A male's voice whispers in broken English.

'No make noise. I help girls,' he reassures me, as I slowly turn around. The man with round, rimless glasses that accentuate his round eyes, points to the olive groves as we make our way in a semi- circle, directed by more cries for help. I'm not sure how my legs are carrying me as I dutifully follow the man, stooping low to avoid detection. As we near the end of the olive grove where the vineyards begin, we don't have as much cover as we crawl on the earth, nearer to the far well. Bile rises in my throat, threatening to release itself onto the ground at the sight of Ruby and Adeline.

Their attacker has his back to us as he turns Ruby to face him and ties her hands with cable ties. Both girls are semi naked as their perpetrator fumbles with the belt on his trousers. The man next to me seems to recognise the girls and their attacker, as his veins pulsate and bulge at his temples. He searches in between the low vines, producing two medium sized stones and hands one to me. He points to where he wants me to attack from, as we pace forward, metres apart, like SAS soldiers. Ruby spots me as she lifts her hands, unable to with the cable ties, in attempt to cover her bare chest. Her face is crimson red as she bows her head to hide her surprise at seeing us. Adeline faces away from us with her ankles tied and her bare back and bottom smeared in dirt.

The man next to me raises his hand and expertly throws the stone at the attacker's head. He turns around, tripping over his trousers as I race forward and throw my full weight at him. The man with glasses spots some cable ties near Ruby's feet and deftly ties one round the attacker's feet, screaming at him as he does so. I reach for another plastic tie and pull his arms up from under him and secure it so hard around his hands, welt marks begin to show.

It all happens so quickly as the man hands me a pocketknife and I untie Ruby and Adeline as they fall to the ground and retrieve their clothing.

'Thank you. Thank you, Manolis, thank you Walter,' Ruby cries as she holds onto a sobbing Adeline. Obviously, they must know the man with glasses as he races back to his pickup truck that has been well hidden in the groves. Within seconds, he screeches back to where he instructs me to help him. With all our strength we haul the attacker, whose body is writhing trying to break free, into the back as I drop the tailgate and Ruby limps over. She spits in the face of her attacker.

'You bastard. I hope you rot in hell!' She then takes his feet and helps us haul him into the truck. In a matter of seconds, the man, who I now know is called Manolis, urges the girls to join him in the front cab while he instructs me to meet them down at the police station in Zante Town. Before I leave, I prop the girl's moped up and move it further into the groves. Now I must try my hardest to follow and keep up with him as his screeches away, as dust clouds obscures my vision. *I wonder what connects the two men?*

Zante Town Police Station

Without hesitation, the attacker is thrown in to a cell into the belly of the austere police station by a group of police officers, who nod in approval at the sight of their latest prisoner.

Manolis, Walter and the girls are led to separate rooms to give statements. A female police officer is appointed to the girls as she carries in two thermal blankets, a jug of lemonade and some pastries.

'Walter, Walter!' Adeline cries as he's just being led into the adjacent room. He turns and smiles. 'Thanks for rescuing us. Don't leave without saying goodbye.' Walter nods his head as a lopsided smile works its way to his cheekbones. It wasn't exactly the plan he had in mind when he first set off this morning with the hope of finding the girls, but in an uncanny kind of way, it's genuinely worked in favour for him, gaining the affection of the lovely Adeline.

'Ruby, Adeline. I am Athena. Firstly, I am so sorry for your attack, but you are safe now. The taxi driver will not be able to breathe the pure air of the island again for a long time. I apologise profusely as he has embarrassed the whole of our island,' the slender police officer explains as she clenches her fists, and her smooth hair sways a little as she shakes her head. Ruby is in awe at her command of the English language as she stays silent. 'I must now ask you to go behind the screen one at a time and remove your underwear. We need to take a swab because of the attack.'

Ruby volunteers first as she mouths *it'll be ok* to her cousin. Adeline slumps down in the softest seat she can find, as adrenaline is replaced with utter exhaustion. The urgent knock on the door startles her as she jumps to her feet as a man in plain clothes enters.

'My cousin is with Athena. She is being examined,' she urges, not wanting the man anywhere near the curtain partition.

'Miss Ruby Royle, I am Detective Sergeant Diamanti. Follow me.'

'No, I'm not Ruby. I am her cousin Adeline.'

Athena pops her head from the partition and nods her head to confirm she has examined Ruby and will now examine Adeline.

In a stuffy, smoke-filled office, D.S. Diamanti offers Ruby a rigid plastic seat and a chipped cup of water. He doesn't trust these tourist girls and is intent on delivering justice to the innocent party. He takes a sip of his thick coffee as he lights a cigarette and then directs his attention to Ruby.

'I have been informed from the Customs at the airport that you have something written in Greek, in the back of your passport. Do you have your passport, Miss Royle?'

Placing her hands on her trembling knees, Ruby takes her passport out of its cover from her day bag and places it on the table with a mixture of dread and relief, as to what the Greek words will reveal, upon translation.

'It seems you like our country, Miss Royle,' the D.S. declares in a monotone voice. Ruby's not sure whether to smile or stay tight lipped as she nods in agreement.

'These words are to inform the Customs when you are in Greece to watch you so that you do not overstay your visa. You have also worked in Athens three years ago, illegally.'

'Is that all?' Ruby cringes as the words flow out of her mouth. 'I mean yes well it was like this...' The D.S. cuts in.

'Miss Royle. I do not think that you realise the importance of these words. To work without a permit is illegal. You are lucky you have not been sent back home when you first arrived here. Also, Miss Royle, your attacker has filed a complaint before he attacked you. He complained that you accosted him when he was protecting our island turtles. He is an activist for their protection and is currently setting up a preservation society. Now this will not be possible. I wish you to leave now.'

They share a harsh stare as Ruby stands to leave. She knows his warning is not to be ignored and that his warning is to leave the island for good, before things escalate.

As Ruby rushes out of his office, desperately trying not to cry, she spots Adeline, Walter and Manolis outside. They huddle together as the low clouds burst, sending rods of rain across the island capital.

She joins them, eager to dispel all thoughts and warnings from the D.S.

'Let's meet tonight. We want to buy you both a meal and drinks. Manolis where do you suggest?' offers Adeline, glad that her cousin has returned.

'Ahh. My uncle has a taverna. I tell him we come at 7pm. Now I must return to my work,' says Manolis as he hands over two business cards with the address on and figures out where he left his pickup.

'Walter. How did you know we were at the wells?' asks Ruby, as she stands there oblivious to the downpour, soaking her to the skin.

'I will tell you the story tonight. Please girls, go back to your hotel and dry off and you should also rest after your attack. I will see you at 7.'

'But Walter, you will definitely be there, won't you?' asks Adeline with a slight crackle in her voice.

6 Revelations and sweet farewells

Taverna Dardanos   Zante Town

'Spiro. How lovely to see you again,' remarks Ruby as she enters the taverna with Walter and Adeline, trying desperately not to jump into his arms. Spiros pumps Walter's hand and pecks the girls on both cheeks.

'Well, what a surprise too Walter,' he enthuses, wondering why his ex- bartender was also involved in the search for the girls.

'Hey, no bad feelings ex- boss,' Walter quips as they take their seat under the plane tree, planted incongruously in the middle of the taverna. The roof has been wound back after the downpour that afternoon, as the stars and moon twinkle above them, shining down like the highest wattage light bulb. The taverna is rustic, with a select menu, specialising in the fruits of the sea, depending on the catch that morning.

'Walter. The minute I told you to leave, I regret it. I was so worried these girls were in danger and you blow your cover too soon, so my hot head got the better of me. And now it turns out my cousin's paranoia was correct, and I thank you and Manolis for your quick actions,' Spiros explains as Walter turns his mouth down and throws back his head a little – a Greek trait he's picked up along the way.

'Talking about Manolis. Where is he?' asks Adeline as she shifts closer to Walter in her chair.

'Ahh, talk to the devil and he is here,' announces Spiros as he beckons his cousin over and he takes his seat. Within minutes, the table is piling up with a plethora of mezes, followed by the freshly caught fish of the day and an ample supply of island wine.

Omitting the horror of the attack, the group discuss their future plans, together with the comical and heart-warming stories that the two cousins share about growing up on a small island together. The local wine flows like a bursting river and voices increase a little in volume, until a familiar figure stumbles past their table and slurs something under his breath. Spiros and Manolis throw their shoulders back in defence as Ruby recognises the huge presence that is D.S. Diamanti. A shiver runs down her spine as she wishes the taverna floor would swallow him up. Spiros takes his cousin's arms to keep him from rising in his seat. Reluctantly, Manolis follows his cousin's wise instructions and continues to break some bread, dipping it in the oil slick that swirls around his plate of fried aubergines and tomatoes.

A few minutes silence ensues around the table as Walter and Adeline excuse themselves to go to the toilets.

'Walter, I know this is crazy and I have never done anything as impulsive as this in my life but after hearing how you came searching for me, I am now certain how I feel. I can't leave. I don't want to go. Oh, hell. Walter what I am trying to say is that I want to stay here with you or anywhere with you. I don't want to leave you,' Adeline blurts out, as they wait for the toilet to become vacant. D.S. Diamanti comes out, fiddling with his flies as Walter reaches for her hand.

'Adeline this is good news. Of course you can stay with me. I just thought you were out of my league – did I say that correct?'

'Yes, you know your English is perfect!' she replies as she takes his other hand and thinks of the words that her cousin has taught her. 'Ik vind je leuk.'

'You like me!' Walter pulls her towards him as a little boy slinks in the toilet before them.

'Come. Let's go and tell them the good news and maybe Spiros will give me my job back and make a job for you,' Walter urges as they forget all about needing the toilet and return to the others.

'Walter, my bartender is a lazy malaka. I am not sure of the word in English. He is too busy looking at the girls in the pool without the bikini tops and he makes shit cocktails. You have your job back.' Spiros beats him to it as they take their seats. Ruby sends her cousin a quizzical look, aware that something profound is going to be announced.

Suddenly the D.S. rises again from the group at his table and this time speaks in English and wags his finger at Ruby, as the man seated next to her tugs at his shoulder.

'You, yes you! English girl. If you stay more than two months on my island there will be trouble for you. Go back to your ugly island. This is our island, not yours.'

Spiros says something in their mother tongue which shuts the D.S. up immediately as he slumps in his chair and downs another tumbler of amber liquid. Ruby goes one better and throws him the back of her hand while his confounded companions snigger into their glasses.

Silence descends as everyone's attention turns to the middle-aged lady at the far side of the taverna.

'She is singing the folk songs from our island. We call them *Kandatha* and the instrument is a mandolin,' whispers Spiros to his table, as Manolis closes his eyes and hums along to the lamentations of the sombre song.

As the musician finishes, she takes a bow and to an astounded Ruby and Adeline, replaces her apron and continues her duties in the kitchen.

The taverna resumes its conversations as Ruby addresses the party.

'I wish I could stay longer than a few more days. Despite our attack, I love your island and its people. And I would just like to raise a toast to our rescuers and protectors, Spiro, Manolis and Walter.'

'Yammas,' they chorus, clinking their glasses together.

Adeline knows that this is the perfect time to reveal her news.

'Ruby, I have some news also. I'm not coming back to England. I have made my mind up and I'm staying here, in the hope that Spiro may offer me a job,' Adeline winks in his direction as he raises his brows and glances at Walter. 'All those times you urged me to come travelling with you Ruby and I was too involved with my career and fiancé at the time. Well now, I want to have a piece of it too. I want to throw all caution to the wind, to not know where my next destination will be. I hope you are happy for me Ruby. Please say something.'

Ruby picks her mouth back of the floor, reaches over the table and squeezes her cousin's hand so hard, Adeline lets out a little yelp.

'Oh my God! Of course I'm happy for you Adeline. But what will your boss say? And your parents?' Ruby enquires, knowing too well her cousin will have thought it all through, even though it seems she has just decided on the spot.

'I hate the bitchy women I work with at the bank, so I was going to change career anyway. I've had enough of sorting everyone else's money problems out. I hate my boss – the epitome of the rich bitch who thinks that wearing a red outfit with outrageously wide shoulder pads portrays power. And as for Mum and Dad! Well, they will just have to be happy for me. At least they still have Veronica with a sparkling career ahead of her and Marcus who will no doubt join my dad's double-glazing firm. So, you see it's all sorted. Goodbye to Adeline Walters the conformist and hello to Adeline the adventurer!'

'I'm completely gobsmacked Addie but of course, in a good way. I'm also a bit envious but I know I need to return home and sort my shit out,' Ruby replies as Spiros strains his ears and looks from girl to girl, to read in between the lines. As she shifts in a little closer to him and their knees touch, Ruby continues.

'I'm happy for all of us. Inadvertently, we have all had a part to play in this strange and eventful holiday. My only regret is endangering the chelona, and I would never have insisted we sleep on the beach that night if I had known about the nesting turtles. But then again, if we hadn't taken the taxi ride, Demetrius would still be at large, preying on some unsuspecting females. And now I can breathe again each time I come to visit Greece, knowing what the words mean in my passport. Plus, tomorrow morning I will be making a complaint about D.S. Diamanti on the grounds of harassment.

'Po, po, po. You are feisty ladies,' Spiros says as he winks at his cousin and allows him to chirp in.

'Ruby, you are correct to report Leonidas Diamanti. We do not like him also. He is an embarrassment like Demetrius Pappas is to our people and island. They are probably related and share the same bad genes,' Manolis adds as he makes a puff sound from his lips. If he were not at the table and with company, he would without doubt, spit on the ground to demonstrate his hatred for Demetrius and Leonidas. His downturned mouth turns upwards as a beautiful woman with dark curly hair slides in the chair next to him and introduces herself as Ariadne, his wife. Unbeknown to Ruby and Adeline, she too has a cause for celebration. The celebration that finally, Demetrius Pappas has got what he deserves.

At the far side of the taverna, the singer come cook, returns to take up her position with her mandolin. Accompanied by her father on the accordion and her son on the tambourine, the taverna erupts with lively music. Manolis and Ariadne are first to take to the dance floor as Spiros takes Ruby's hand, followed by Walter and Adeline, urging them to join in.

'Ela, Ela, we dance the Sirtos. This is our island dance.'

There's not an inch to move on the dance floor as the girls and Walter are taught the intricate moves by Manolis and Ariadne. The night is filled with laughter and love, as dance after dance, the happy group form a bond, sealed by fate one balmy August night.

Early the next morning, Ruby wakes up in an unfamiliar room. She's back at the Angel Hotel, alone in a double bed. Spiros is on his terrace awaiting Maria from the Minimart to deliver the breakfast.

The table is laid, and the coffee is in a flask keeping warm. The sun is still low and the temperature bearable. When she realises where she is, Ruby slips on her dress from the previous evening and joins him on the terrace, a minute before Maria climbs the metal stairs, mischievous smile lighting up her face. Mari knows of Spiro's past heartache and knows he has grieved long enough..

The previous evening, Spiros offered to take the girls and Walter to the airport. Not knowing where Adeline is, once they have eaten, they take a chance and hope they will make their own way to the airport.

Time is ticking by as he urges Ruby to gather her small bag and climb into the cab of his pickup.

On the way back to Zante Town, Ruby feels she is losing a good friend as she sits for the last time next to Spiros and breathes in his masculine scent.

'Ruby. I need to warn you of something,' he says, looking into her eyes.

'Oh dear. Spit it out then Spiro.' Ruby pre-empts his words, but they are not the words she was dreading.

'Ruby. Although I do not like the man, I think it is wise not to report D.S. Leonidas Diamanti when we arrive at the police station to pick up your passport. He is a very influential person on the island, in both good and in not so good ways.

However, I must admit, although I think he is a leopard with spots he does not change, there is a caring side to him. What is happening is this: Now that Demetrius Pappas is detained in the cells, he has asked for the help of D.S. Diamanti. He may be feeling that he wants to make good his guilty conscience, so he says he has been trying to set up a preservation fund for some years for our special Caretta Caretta chelonas of the island. He says to the D.S. that, because of his amnesia, it is difficult for him, but now he is in the cell, it is even harder.' Ruby interrupts.

'But how do you know all this Spiro? You have been with me all last night.' She twiddles her hair around her finger as she looks out of the where a couple of young women stride up the road, nearly tripping over their clumsy suitcases.

'Ahh, this is the privilege of living on a small island. Everyone is a brother, sister or cousin of someone. My sister cleans the station and hears a lot of hushed conversations and sees a lot of documents carelessly left on desks.

'Oh right. Carry on please Spiro.' Ruby

'So, I will tell you what my sister told me this morning but please never say anything to anyone that my sister looks at the papers.'

'Don't worry Spiro. Of course I won't, but please carry on as we haven't much time.'

'My sister noticed a letter from Demetrius Pappas, the malaka who attacked you. It was to the D.S. Diamanti. He asks for the D.S. to act for him to raise money on the island to be able to set a preservation fund around the bay of Laganas and Kalamaki, to protect the chelona. I am not sure how this will be done with the laws of the island and bureaucracy, but I think it will be good for the island and good for making Demetrius Pappas into a better man.'

Ruby's conscience gets the better of her as a solitary tear runs down her cheek. If only she had done her homework on the island about the Loggerhead turtles! Thankfully, Spiros does not see her despair as he stops outside the police station and waits for her while she retrieves her troublesome passport.

The Airport

'Well, this is it Ruby. I never thought our one-week holiday would be so life changing. Have you decided what you are going to do back home yet?' Adeline asks as she reaches for a tissue in her bag.

'Well, I will probably sob into my pillow wishing I was back here with you but then I will have a good talk to myself and tell myself I need to grow up and focus on a career. I'm not sure just what yet, but maybe some degree that will involve travel and tourism so I can live in the sun all year round. Oh, and I might just have a letter from the guy from Warrington. If he's back from India, I might just see how the land lies there. Either way, I'm determined to go to University and you never know, I might be able to pop back over here in the holidays and hang out with you two lovebirds - at the Angel Hotel and Zero's bar!' Ruby answers as they move further into the airport departure lounge.

'It's so uncanny isn't it Ruby? You know, how our roles have reversed. Here's me being reckless, abandoning my career and all I've ever known, and you becoming all sensible!'

The time has arrived for Ruby to go through Customs and present her passport. The cousins hug each other tight as Walter and Spiros look on, realising just how strong the bond is between them. As they eventually release their hold, the two men step forward. Walter makes the first move as he shakes Ruby's hand, as she pulls him in for a bear hug.

'Ruby, you need to come back anyway to finish off your ride around the island with Adeline. And if you will allow me to follow you again on the moped, we can finally make it over to Navagio Beach and the famous shipwreck.'

'Oh hell! The moped. We forget to take it back. We left it at the wells,' Ruby announces as Walter explains,

'Ruby, don't worry, Theodore has already picked it up and there's no damage done.'

As Ruby nods in agreement, Walter moves to one side allowing Spiros to say farewell. As he takes her hand in his, they both lean a little closer, as Ruby tunes into his urgent whisper,'

'Ruby if you miss your cousin and my island, I can make a job for you at the Angel Hotel. I think you know what I want to say.'

She nods and tips her head to the side as she drowns in his sensual eyes, remembering their evening on the beach then noticing his quirky curly moustache as he twirls it around his little finger in contemplation.

'I might just hold you to that,' she replies as she plants a lingering kiss on his cheek and reluctantly releases her hold on him. She knows the serene look on his face will be etched in her memory for quite some time.

Disappearing around the flimsy partition, he blows her a kiss and she catches it, putting it in her pocket to save for letter.

She hands the Customs officer her passport. He scrutinises the back page, looks her up and down, clicks his tongue, hands it back to her and waves her on.

The End

A note from the author

This novella was inspired by my adoration for the Greek Islands. Although fictional, it is loosely based on events and observations from a holiday with my cousin in Zante/Zakynthos, way back in 1990, where we were both enamoured and intrigued with the miraculous Loggerhead turtles (chelona). In 1990, Laganas main strip was untarmacked!

Who's who

Main characters in order of appearance:

Ruby Royle: cousin to Adeline

Adeline Walters: cousin to Ruby

Demetrius Pappas: taxi driver at the airport and features in the back story

The Chelona turtles

Manolis Papadimitriou : owner of the pest control business, gives Ruby and Adeline a lift from Kalamaki and features in the back story

Spiro Angelo: owner of the Hotel Angel and cousin to Manolis

Walter: bartender at the Hotel Angel

Maria: works in the MiniMart

Ariadne Papadimitriou : wife of Manolis and features in the back story

D.S. Diamanti: questions Ruby at the police station

Social media: Instagram: elisewilliamsnovels

Novels and novellas to date:

Debut novel

Going Upside Down – set in Australia

The Grecian Adventures collection:

A Lock up On Crete

Finding my Feet on Crete

Ariadne Papadimitriou : wife of Manolis and features in the back story

D.S. Diamanti: questions Ruby at the police station

Social media: Instagram: elisewilliamsnovels

Novels and novellas to date:

Debut novel

Going Upside Down – set in Australia

The Grecian Adventures collection:

A Lock up On Crete

Finding my Feet on Crete

There's Something about Athens

There's Something about Zante

The Italian Adventures collection:

There's Something about Naples – coming soon (March – April 2025)

Printed in Great Britain
by Amazon